PRAISE FOR GARRETT COOK

"Written with the haunting lyricism of early Clive Barker and with the poetic prowess of Kathe Koja, Garrett Cook's *Charcoal* is an elegantly beguiling tone poem of trauma and suffering. To miss out on this masterpiece would be to miss out on watching a master craftsman at work. An utterly bewitching read."

— ERIC LAROCCA, AUTHOR OF *THINGS HAVE GOTTEN WORSE SINCE WE LAST SPOKE*

"With echoes of Rimbaud and Baudelaire, Garrett Cook's poetic, lyrical *Charcoal* explores with a licentious butcher's cruel insight the bloody thread that connects the darkness in man, the darkness in the medium by which art is created, and the darkness in art itself."

— MATTHEW M. BARTLETT, AUTHOR OF *GATEWAYS TO ABOMINATION*

"*Charcoal* nails the pain that every artist knows — the agony of creation and the despair of grasping for recognition — and lays it bare on the page, naked and shrieking, like nothing before."

— BITTER KARELLA, HUGO AWARD NOMINATED CREATOR OF THE MIDNIGHT SOCIETY TWITTER

T0025797

"To miss Garrett Cook's book would be to miss a singular vision of horror akin to early Clive Barker with the permeating hopelessness of Scott Smith's *The Ruins* or Cormac McCarthy's *The Road*."

— BOOK AUTOPSY

"Garrett Cook commands gratuity and psychological horror like no one else I've read."

— NATHAN CARSON, DRUMMER FOR WITCH MOUNTAIN, AUTHOR OF *STARR CREEK*

"A whirlpool of consciousness, smoothly drawing you in and then sweeping you along in ever-faster tightening spirals to plunge into a dark, mind-blowing vortex."

— CHRISTINE MORGAN, AUTHOR OF *LAKEHOUSE INFERNAL*, SPLATTERPUNK AWARD WINNER

"*Charcoal* expertly weaves different levels of reality, going from past to present to canvas to dream."

— JOE KOCH, AUTHOR OF *THE WINGSPAN OF SEVERED HANDS*

"*Charcoal* is full of brilliant darkness and on-point observations about people, trauma and the ways we interact with problematic art. Gothic, nightmarish, and feels very much like falling into a historic painting of hell."

— MADELEINE SWANN, AUTHOR OF *THE SHARP END OF THE RAINBOW*

CHARCOAL

GARRETT COOK

CL◄SH

To Sophia
for helping me live and thrive again

To Oscar Wilde, Edvard Munch and Val Lewton
for inspiration

To whoever comes next when I am gone

CONTENTS

CHARCOAL

REBIRTH OF VENUS

I n the first panel of the triptych, a naked woman is laid out upon a divan. She claws at a face covered in burns and awkward stitching alike, stripping skin from it and bringing streaks of blood down. There is no pain upon that face, only an expression of pure surrender. Though party to her own scarification, she is content and in fact, ecstatic. This first panel of the triptych is famously entitled "Venus Reborn".

BOSTON 2021

DANCERS

There is a place in the place behind the eyes so blighted and barren that the only thing that grows there is the scream. You can salt the Earth (and for sure the Earth there is salted) and the scream for sure can grow. And it can emerge and tell you to take no shit from the cashier or to drink ten beers and fall over, ready to choke to death on them and all the other things that you forced down to keep alive. There is not much that can live alongside the scream. Sometimes we ourselves cannot. If asked if she could, Shannon might have answered no but the thing that grew beside the scream, it answered yes.

There were things that had tried to squeak by and make her honest. They had tried to say to paint the party before they came and answered "what party?" and tried to make born the things she'd seen through heavy eyes as alien weight pressed on and instead she said "what party?" and the scream drowned out the need to say anything but "what party?" Something else needed to happen, the brush needed to bring other life.

It was a shape like a person, red, bombastic, arms outstretched in joy and receptivity and readiness. It was moving to imaginary music; not just moving, in fact but moved as well. Though born in sepulchral silence, it stretched out in ecstasy, this red blob of a person and danced to the front of her eyes out from behind them. She had tried to fade into the dark but she was not alone there, since now there was this red creature with her, exuberant and moving to a rhythm she could not hear.

She picked up her brush and squeezed out her paints, and on the canvas she let this figure, this companion in her loneliness be born there, ablaze with kinetic energy and with a joie de vivre that she could not find in herself. She could not quite live as she lived but this red thing, whatever the fuck and whoever the fuck it was had been granted permission to dance. As it was created, she could feel something altogether alien; she could feel it was thankful for life. She wondered how it had gotten there and what it was to feel something like that. It had been a long time since that sensation had gone and left; it was not that she was outright suicidal but only that she did not perceive life as doing her any particular favors. How did this red mass of kinetic energy born now onto the canvas get to this place?

And then a second voice resounded from that place behind the eyes and it longed for life and what it offered, it longed to explore and know and to love. She had these feelings sometimes when they weren't choked back by distress, loss, distrust, and disloyalty. The blue one emerged from that place and held out open arms for its red compatriot, dancers as they both were. She conjured up not what she felt at the moment but what she wished to feel and what she wished was still known to her. Maybe she could be like that and maybe she could know them again. She let it be born and show her this and maybe another who looked at the painting could feel it in the open arms of the blue one.

And what if beyond being open, one could flourish, one could be adroit and graceful and float? What if one could walk about the hostile and unjust Earth and dare to try and transcend? What if one could not only walk or run but leap and in leaping, one could aspire then to fly? She thought often about her "work ethic" but not about excellence and not about genius and not about the miraculous. She was trying to just do her shit and keep her head down and get good but with the red and blue shapes emerging, she felt in touch with a long-suppressed wish and that wish was to rise above. The yellow shape leapt eternal into the painting and in its leaping, it rose and it would rise and rise and rise and rise...yes, this was nice and worth it. This was going to happen for her.

But when one rises, one will surely descend and when they descend, what is there? The ground is not just or merciful and does not care if you live through it. The ground is thirsty for your brains and guts and the splinters of bone and scraps of you that it can soak up since you've fallen and fallen down dead. The hopes you had when rising are there to fight the grumbling in its guts, its ground guts, the furnace in the center of the Earth, and gives heat to all things and people there and it wants those desires to keep the furnace going to run the gears that grind us into what we are and what we are is that which does not rise without having to face the knowledge that it will plummet.

But what if we fell and when we fell, there was a set of hands and there was nothing for the greedy Earth to slurp? What if somebody wished we would not fall? But they'd need not be asked again beyond the act of catching and we would not need them to be there and do more than they do, which is the simple act of catching? This, oh, this, would it be too much to ask or was there a way that such a creature could spring into existence and sprung from there could catch and we wouldn't fall and we wouldn't need to ask because it gets so hard to ask and they won't if you ask and they won't know and they mustn't know...

But the green one, it extended arms and thought only for the glory of the yellow and what the yellow would find up there when it rose. There was something to be said for that and there was much relief to be had knowing it was born and since it was born, it wanted others to rise and if they should come down to come down only with stories and convey then the feeling of the sky and the infinite above and the infinite above even that. There could be such a thing and there was proof because that thing had been born and could do what it was born to do. It was ready and because it was, there could be ascension. The Earth grumbled its dissent and it didn't matter. She felt happy painting this.

Her friend Rem walked in from the hallway, happy to see that something again was happening on the easel that had of late been lonely and empty as the woman whose dorm it resided in. Rem dressed, acted and walked like gender was a thing they had fought, argued their way to the other side of and sauntered in, looking disquietingly fine in a half shirt adorned with Warhol's face and a pair of tight shorts adorned with everybody's gaze. And though Rem wanted to encourage their friend, Rem had been afflicted with something fierce; beyond being born uncertain of where they stood among their fellow humans, Rem was born honest. Rem had been drawn to Shannon for being fiercely independent and for being creative and having great potential to reveal inner truths that would cut you to the bone, that is, if that potential was met. Rem felt good that Shannon was painting but felt mad at what Shannon WAS painting. Shannon had been evasive, canceled plans, mumbled and trailed off when important shit came up.

"Wow, somewhere a Boys and Girls Club is missing its mural."

Shannon was freed from the reverie of making. Shannon was now looking at a canvas and on that canvas, Shannon saw what she desired and what she dreamed of but what she couldn't see was how things were and what she couldn't see when she looked at it was how she would make that world happen and how she could make herself believe it could. These figures had crawled forth from a void and now when she saw the figures she saw not space but the space where the figures in that space had come from and how they could fill that dark with something lovely to look at and still reflect the truth. She was brought back to the world by Rem the friend, the crush, the fabulous ass, the bold pronouns and the unassailable attitude. She hadn't been out much since Wyatt's party, so when she started to create, she created with nobody else in mind.

"Holy shit," said Rem. Rem was going to blame the sativa but was mortified enough that they didn't stop and think about it.

"That came out wrong."

No dancing. No holding. No leaping. Nobody to catch. She hadn't been dancing, she hadn't drawn someone close. She hadn't sought to rise above expectations and get to a place she'd never been where she could do things she would never do and then if she did them wrong, then things could be fine again and when they were fine then maybe they'd stay fine but nothing but nothing stays fine because the Earth is thirsty for us and it needs the guts and brains we splat out so it can keep going and grinding us all the way down. We disconnect and flee back to the empty easel and the things we can't talk about. There are so many things that we just don't talk about.

"No, Rem," she said, "I want you to call me on my shit, okay? It's important that you call me on my shit."

"I'm still an asshole," said Rem, "still sorry."

"Well, shit, Rem," said Shannon, "it's not like I didn't know."

Her phone on the coffee table lit up. Text from Wyatt. She was not going to answer a text from Wyatt right now. She didn't want to see him.

"You'd be dumb as this fucking painting if you didn't," said Rem, noting that Shannon's gaze had shifted to the phone. They decided that Shannon needed a distraction.

"Weren't we watching The OC?" Rem asked. "I can't believe you'd never seen it."

Shannon shrugged.

"Too many white people."

"Couple cis ones too," Rem shot back, "is there beer?"

There was beer.

LONDON 1885

THE LIBERTINE

On the walls of Thomas Kemp's drawing room, there hung paintings of men with giant red noses and sullen eyes that begged release from some indefinable malady, one that they would never live without. On the walls, there hung women whose sunken chests and sharp, almost cruel breasts promised nothing but disappointment and heartbreak and whose wan, cadaverous faces showed that the life they would lie and steal and pander for was barely there, the vampiresses not plump on the blood of victims, not even sustained by it. There could be comparisons to Egon Schiele or Goya but these paintings went beyond simply searching out the ugliness and vulnerability of their subjects to an outright spitting contempt for them.

The drawing room, indeed, the house had been inherited from a family who had appointed it with opulent fabrics, expensive furnishings and artifacts from throughout the colonies. There were places for the guests' eyes to focus but it was difficult to avoid Kemp's handiwork which left Branwell and Mrs. Mulberry alike feeling disquieted. Kemp was to most an unpleasant obligation and to others an amusing curiosity. The young man of good breeding who had decided to put his dislike of most everyone onto a canvas was a frequent topic of discussion but seldom one of inquiry. Branwell, however, counted Kemp as a friend and did his best to try and understand the poor misanthrope.

"What I don't understand, Kemp, is why a man like yourself should bother to paint. You don't need the money from selling paintings, and if you did, you would be most unfortunate. I couldn't imagine thinking I could make a living off of the ghastly things you make."

Kemp huffed. He regretted that he had gathered his so called friends here in his drawing room for drinks. He needed to remind himself more often that these gatherings seldom went well for him.

"I'm not interested in dancing girls or bowls of fruit. If I wish to look every day upon a bowl of fruit, I will simply have a bowl brought to me."

"Yes," said Branwell, "and it is within your means to do this. A man like yourself shouldn't take up the arts because he knows his belly will be full. Everyone knows great art comes from suffering."

Branwell was young, rich and considered handsome because of his sandy hair, cool blue eyes and lean, athletic build. His nose was rather too long and one of his legs was shorter than the other. He had lost a tooth in a boxing match during his school days and because of this, he smiled with his mouth shut and nobody noticed this when they looked upon him. He was a terrible bore and would share the terrible poems he composed at parties to the applause and pleasure of the young ladies who considered him a great prospect for a husband. Branwell was one to talk about artistic ambitions held by men without life experience. How splendid it would be to take from him more of those teeth!

"Such a paradox," said Mrs. Mulberry, "that we should become patrons of the arts and make artists comfortable and then when they are comfortable, they cease to be inspired."

Kemp examined the blueblooded bitch. He saw that her shoulders were wide and dimpled and she was squeezed too tight into her dress and that the corset could not hold back the pendulous gut of the well fed. Her face was asymmetrical and her forehead was developing wrinkles. There was a wart on her left middle finger and her laugh was like the yowling of a cat. Kemp regarded her and felt himself dying, losing the moments he spent in her company, rotting where he stood and growing dumber from the inanities spewing from her surprisingly crooked mouth.

"Well, my dear Mrs. Mulberry," said Kemp, "I fear you are in the wrong, for you assume me to know nothing at all of pain. That couldn't be further from the truth."

"You're from a good family," said Branwell, "your inheritance is quite sizable. Your home is spacious and comfortable, you are warm and well fed while others starve and grow ill. You are, as far as I can see, sane and seldom suffering melancholy. So, please, Thomas, do tell us what hardships a man like yourself has been through."

Kemp emptied the brandy decanter into a water glass.

"I shall tell you, Branwell, that I know very much about hardship and agony. My eyes must suffer the toadlike flesh of aristocratic matrons and the dreadful verse of shallow and insufferable twits. Your friendship feels venomous, your features so distinct and handsome are simply another kind of hideousness. I suffer because I am not understood and because I do not desire to be. I suffer because life has nothing that brings me joy, save for the momentary sensation that I have rendered in paint, how terrible you all are and how much I wish to be left alone, even if, while left alone, I am forced to face myself in the mirror and to live with my own ugliness. The hacking cough of a tradesman is in comparison a rather small inconvenience."

Branwell looked upon Kemp with pity and disdain all at once, a look that was not unfamiliar to the young artist. Kemp's company was hard to keep, as hard to maintain as his attention and as difficult as his art. There was in him genius and a certain amount of clarity for certain but Kemp's suffering was indeed quite contagious and while he wished that Mrs. Mulberry and her like were more often given short shrift, he felt the opinions of his friend did not engender shame in those who would be shameful but condescension in those who felt that etiquette was a sign of intellect and value.

"Maybe," said Branwell, "the world is an absolute cesspool and placing life upon its surface was a great misjudgement for a capricious and terrible god who loves us not. Maybe it was not for us to erect cities but to squat in caves fending for our lives with sharp, flint knives. There are many fine writers and fine philosophers who have said such a thing, so I would not dare claim credit. There is likely some veracity in all that. But there is also another possibility that may exist distinctly from this one and would not negate it in the slightest. It is possible that there is a fine and clear reason that you suffer as you do and you feel it to be as distinct and acute as you do."

Kemp gulped down much of the brandy, feeling no particular burn or discomfort from it.

"Please, do go on, Branwell. I am so very interested in your insights, no doubt honed as sharp as can be."

"It is possible that you are a miserable shit. And that you are such a miserable shit you can't imagine anyone would choose to be anything but a miserable shit. Perhaps we should pity you then."

Kemp went out into the night and found no friends, no comfort, not a trace of anything to move him or prove him wrong. In the pubs, the sailors and tradesmen of Whitechapel were carousing but Kemp was simply drinking. He could no longer remember if it was he who declined companionship and intimate friendship or if the world had refused his kinship first, told him he was so hideous and shameful that nothing wished to reflect back upon him. The night was chill and stagnant and the skies were choked with fog and smog, providing him no ease and no answers and no peace. He had expected none, but in his chilly, stagnating heart, he longed for them.

Kemp did not think to buy the barroom a round or to ask where the night would take them. He examined the whores of the East End and he found only disgust. He did not wish to fuck or paint them. There were impulses, worse ones, screeches of antisocial suggestions that he drowned out with his fear of acting upon such things and inflicting harm. He was above these wretched beasts but this did not mean he would soil himself with their blood or any other fluids for that matter. He told those voices and thoughts to be silent and leave him be.

The city had nothing for him but in his room at least, there was something that would put him at ease and let him pass another night. He sat down at the desk and opened the top drawer slowly. As much as he took comfort in the pistol, he dreaded it as well. Kemp dreaded his own thoughts sometimes, distracting voices that conspired against silence and solitude, which were Kemp's preference over noise and clamor and company. Kemp could not think of the pistol without thinking why he had purchased it in the first place and why night after night, he would take it out and look at it and reflect on the freedom it could represent.

There were nights, like this one, wherein Kemp's fear of the pistol was conquered by his fascination for it. With the pistol in his hand, he would have had a very different conversation with Branwell. Branwell would have started his condescending comments and then Kemp would have grabbed the pistol and put a bullet into the bastard's heart. And then as Branwell hit the floor clutching his chest, Mrs. Mulberry would fall to the floor, clutching her own, dead of a heart attack, and that would show them for ridiculing his work and treating him like some sort of deranged child.

But in truth, Kemp would miss this man. He would be left to the company of whores and fops and artists he'd thrown money at to paint uninteresting scenes of dance halls and bowls of fruit and the very aristocrats he tried to avoid. Kemp, without Mrs. Mulberry or without Branwell was a man alone with his gun and the strangers on the streets he most unbecomingly frequented and perhaps worst of all, with the hideousness in the mirror. He turned and shifted Branwell's face into dimensions that made it as foul as he was used to but it did little good. He could not paint, he could not sleep and he could not make use of his beloved pistol.

There were many nights like this in the life of Thomas Kemp, whom history would come to know as the Libertine. To be piteous does not make one beyond contempt. To be pitied does not mean one is not to be feared. It was a pitiful thing, his almost nightly conversation with the gun, a sign of emptiness and isolation. Though he felt alone in these feelings and thought that his suffering was special and acute, it was not. He could see the ugliness and desperation and vulnerability in those he painted but could not for even a second think that they were like him in their loneliness or more to the point that he was anything like them. Thomas Kemp was meant to be alone. To the misfortune of many, this did not mean that he would be.

He would find what he thought was love with an actress. She would fawn over his paintings. She would lose his attention and adoration. She would beg him to touch her, to love her, to remember her. He would tell her that her beauty sickened him because it would. It would make him feel ignorant and hollow and wrong about the world. In tears, she would come before him with a knife in her hand and she would make sure her face never offended him again. In the wake of this, he would love her as he never had before, but only because he got from this his first truly great work of art.

SLIDES

Rem's words came like a brick thrown through the window of a man's reputation as an academic. Though short, they thundered like barbarous hoofbeats down a mountain, waiting to sack this small outpost of strongjawed tweed patched metrosexual Prius driving white cis upmarket art school bullshit.

"You've got to be fucking kidding me."

If Rem regretted saying this out loud to Professor Jameson, Shannon found no evidence that they did. Professor James was a creep and deserved about this much respect, if not less. but that of course did not mean that he would get that little respect. No matter how many grad student girlfriends he brought, unashamed, to faculty events or how often his eyes had found their way down blouses or up skirts, he had his reputation, his following and beyond that, he had tenure. Shannon felt a flush of thirst. She hated herself for the two years of flirting back with this dude.

"Here we go," said a green-haired, noseringed twenty-six-year-old who had tried to pick Shannon up a couple times. She did not remember the name of this poseur acolyte who had provided the devil much pro bono counseling. She did not care to know it, since she did not care to know him. Nosering had been kicked off Twitch for cumtribbing photos of Ilhan Onmar on stream. She'd seen him socially at one of Wyatt's parties but would cross the street to avoid him or the GI Joes he had melted to a canvas to spell out "faggot".

"What's that supposed to mean?" Shannon snapped at him. She knew she would immediately regret it.

"This always comes up with you SJWs," Nosering replied, "everybody has to be squeaky clean or you dykes cancel their ass. Artists aren't squeaky clean, they're rebels."

Shannon and Rem did not get on especially well with Marcela, a purveyor of dull geometries and "is it art?" red blotches in the middle of canvases but Marcela nonetheless got involved and they were nonetheless grateful because it meant another occasion where they weren't.

"You can be a rebel without keeping women hostage in your basement," Marcela shot back at Nosering. In Shannon's eyes, she kind of gained a few points from that. It was nice not to feel alone and surrounded by assholes, even if this feeling would no doubt subside when the professor opened his mouth.

"That was never proven," said Professor Jameson, "and you have to remember that Kemp existed in a time where those who made unpleasant art or had unconventional sexual tastes were assumed to be criminals or deviants. Rumors surrounded a lot of people like Kemp but that doesn't mean that he was capable of doing the things he was accused of."

"But there are other artists we could…"

Shannon was not surprised that she was interrupted.

"Other artists who made different art, none of which holds a candle to the Unfinished Triptych. We are not covering those artists because they didn't do these great paintings that we are going to be looking at and analyzing and discussing. Whoever Thomas Kemp was or wasn't doesn't determine the value of his contributions to the arts and it doesn't change what we as artists and scholars can learn from his work. The Kemp estate was good to this school and gave us some very valuable prints and antiques. We all know about the box."

Shannon had read the accounts of that woman in the basement. She had read of her feelings of weakness and insignificance and the degradation she had suffered. She had seen in this woman's suffering her own and in this woman's life the desperation of every woman whose voice was unheard or negated. She had seen in Evelyn a symbol of truth that would not be suppressed and dignity and strength that could survive anything no matter how much had been taken. She had tried to internalize that but could not find that in herself. She shouldn't have needed to be brave but she needed to be brave.

"If we treat him like it didn't happen, then he gets away with it."

Professor Jameson put up a wagging finger.

"Ah. So you think we become accomplices in the artist's depravity?"

Shannon squirmed in her seat. She had brought more attention upon herself than she wanted. She had to remain unnoticed most of the time, conscious of her blackness and their whiteness and wanting to melt into the room. But this was not to be today. It was usually just his eyes. She suddenly feared his hands, his affection. She may have initiated a game that she did not wish to play while trying to disengage from work she did not wish to witness or experience. She wished there were ways to keep men like him from thinking she was engaging in more than the material. She wished now that she had not gotten mad.

"I asked a question, Miss Hernandez."

Shannon forced out an answer though she knew she would regret it.

"Yes, I think maybe we are."

Shannon was beaned in the temples by the sensation that she was about to get "owned". This could mean she'd been met by a superior argument or could mean the conversation would progress to something that she could only dignify with physical force or projectile vomiting.

"Do you consider yourself superstitious?"

Was he being racist or just generally weird? It was difficult to tell.

"No, I don't think I'm superstitious."

The professor brought out an easel with a big sketch pad on it. This was weird because the screen was already down for projecting slides.

"The arts sometimes make people superstitious, Miss Hernandez. The images and ideas we're presented with are infectious. They can change our minds or our hearts or sometimes our character if we're not careful. It's witchcraft of a sort, using words and symbols to try and transform the audience and force them to connect with something they had no intention of connecting with. It's very scary. We risk a lot by exposing ourselves to influences like these. Particularly when they come from people we're afraid of."

She got what he was getting at but did not like where it was going. She wanted to be literally anywhere else right now. Safe. Invisible. Smaller and smaller until the prying eyes and grasping hands could never find her again. Let me unsay it. Let me hide, please let me hide.

"I guess."

The professor opened his desk drawer, pulling out a mahogany box.

"Do you know what's in this box?"

Shannon's heart froze at the sight of it. There was no good reason to be afraid and yet that did not matter. It couldn't be what the art department said it was. The story couldn't have been true in the first place and the idea that they had been donated these charcoals by an alumnus made it even less likely. The box was still frightening and the box was still full of something that he was bringing out to prove a point through some form or another of public humiliation.

"It's supposedly charcoals with Kemp's ashes mixed in. I'm not even sure that's physically possible."

The professor smiled condescendingly.

"Yes, it's rumored that Kemp had his ashes mixed with these charcoals and that they have lasted over a century. They're a priceless artifact. The sort of thing I wouldn't bring into class to share if they were what they supposedly are. It's rumored that Kemp did this. It was part of his myth, like all the other stories about him. They're all equally implausible."

Shannon shook her head.

"I don't think that's true."

"Stand up, Miss Hernandez. Come to the easel."

She wasn't going to fight it. Fighting had gotten her to this point already. Nosering was laughing into his hands. Marcela was mortified for her and had withdrawn her support. She approached the professor.

"Miss Hernandez, these ideas have power over us only to the extent that we let them. The charcoals in this box could have been bought last night at Dick Blick and switched out or they could be made with the bones of a kidnapper and sorcerer. It's your choice how you take in a new idea or a piece of art and what you let it do to you."

The professor opened the box and handed her one of the charcoals. She took it, breathing in deep as she did. This did not feel right. It could be the humiliation, it could be the myth, it could be the tainted attention of a man she really did not want but it did not feel right to have this in her hand, even if it was just from Dick Blick. She hoped he would make whatever point he was making quickly so she could put this damn thing down and sit again.

"If you're not superstitious and you don't believe that this has power over you, then I want you to go to the easel and draw with it."

She nodded and approached the easel. Her hands shook, fingers stained with black something. It was charcoal. It was only charcoal, purchased from Dick Blick a week before, to make a point. Squirming inside from expectant eyes, she lifted her hand to make the first stroke on the sketch pad, wondering if she was indeed making use of a treasured heirloom just so this obnoxious prick could make a point about art and ethics. Such a fucking creep. She powered through and forced herself to draw.

She made a circle, looking from the professor to the class to see if they were content that she had done this and proven that she was not afraid even though she was and had no reason to be ashamed of it. They wanted her to carry on. They needed her to do more and to fill this empty page with something, no matter what it was. She kept scribbling around the circle, unsure of herself and of what she was giving birth to through those scribbles. There couldn't have been any standards but she still feared she wouldn't meet them.

She scribbled more, another circle around it, spirals into spirals into spirals. Time stood still as she surrounded that outer ring with even more circles, feverishly scribbling, defiantly scribbling, rebelling with her compliance to rebel. She left herself as she often left herself, again at a place of fear and violation that she no longer needed to be there for. She could be free of this and it was better that she be free. It was always better that she be free.

She returned from this sojourn away only when summoned back by the sound of applause, perhaps sarcastic from the professor and from the class. Back in herself, she observed the admiration, genuine or otherwise and she accepted it, even as she was still afraid and repulsed and bothered and ready to leave and drop the class and go who fucking knows where.

"Well done, Miss Hernandez," said the professor, "you showed me that you weren't afraid to engage, even if it means literally getting your hands dirty. That's not nothing, you know. Everybody here can learn from that and you can learn from that bravery as we look into the paintings."

His hand was on her shoulder. His platitudes felt fake but his touch felt real and slimy. The charcoal felt right in her hand and she hesitated to return it to the box with its brethren, Dick Blick or cremains or whatever they might have been. She thanked him politely and returned to her seat as he started up the projector to show the slides.

The paintings they saw were ghastly and they could have been the work of a kidnapper, a torturer or just a rampaging misogynist. She should have been more unsettled for all the arguing she'd done but her attention instead kept wandering over to the sketch pad and the marks she had drawn on it.

They were harmless scribbles, just circles inside of circles inside of circles. Nothing but blackness on the page and on her fingers. It should have felt like nothing but after a few minutes of staring, she could swear that she saw something there.

Small, indistinct, barely a part of the picture. Still, it was there and when she spotted it, she couldn't ignore it. She hadn't thought she'd drawn a face.

CROWS

There were some who said that the man who cremated Thomas Kemp smothered his own infant in his crib. They say that he had heard a voice which told him that the Earth was the devil's domain and that this baseborn boy would see hardship, poverty and abuse above all else. The voice would go on to tell him that a parent can do nothing so kind as to liberate their offspring from an indignant Earth and prevent them from knowing what it is to live in the cruel, debased realm of matter under the bitter gaze of the nemesis of God. He would comply and beneath a pillow, the child would find freedom from the myriad ails of which life was composed.

They say when this man's wife came home, she looked on his works, mouth agape and asked him why he had done that which he'd just done and received from him a long and thorough refutation of the virtues of life on Earth. He had never read philosophy, he had never attended lectures on the subject and he had certainly never unleashed such a polysyllabic assault on the kindness of the Almighty but he took right to it and in her present vulnerable state, she found truth in his words and begged him to take her life. He complied, choking her to death.

Now alone and faced with the realities of his actions, there was but one thing to do. Impatient, unable to take another moment of life so cruel and unfair and devoid of potential, he picked up a knife and slit his own throat. The story said it only took contact with Kemp's remains to drive this man to suicidal and homicidal fervor. The story said his wickedness had seeped into his body and passed onto this man, spreading a crude Manichaeism that could lead only to murder.

That story was only a myth from a time when such things were harder to verify. It had been told at parties by Crowley, Blavatsky and years later, Orson Welles, Jimmy Page and Grant Morrison. Popular though it was, it had been untrue and a sanitization of a colder and harsher truth about the ashes of Thomas Kemp, the Libertine.

The cruelty and perversity of Thomas Kemp was not kept in his bones. It was not so clean as that. If we keep our hands off Polanski's clapboard and OJ's gloves, ghost stories tell us that we shall remain untainted by their poisons. The cruelty of Thomas Kemp was in his legend, in the words of those who said libertine instead of monster, iconoclast instead of brute, philosopher instead of madman. The cruelty of Thomas Kemp was in the charcoal because the ground he'd tended had been salted down and henceforth could be tended but with blood.

And with the ecstasy of circles feverishly scribbled and connecting to that shameless past, she began to feel that connection, the hand that guides, the eyes that judge, the face beneath. There on that canvas, hidden on those dark spirals, she had called that face beneath.

There are words we speak that are only larval howls, destined for short life as caterwaul before dying on the ears of a listener assailed. They begin as impulses under words, growing into breath and come out as attempts to communicate. They hounded, plagued and chased her, they led her back to the professor's office and asking if she could try them out again for a bit. She smiled big, exploited the eyes he'd stared into, flirted though he had filled her with contempt and revulsion, and on these vague promises that made her feel filthy, she brought the charcoals home for a week.

At first, they had felt wrong in her hands. They were

rough, awkward and they left smudges on her fingers. They were imprecise compared to pencils or brushes, forcing her to make wider strokes. Where the oils she was used to came in a myriad of colors, the charcoals were irrevocably black. Insincere though they were, the dancing figures evoked a multitude of feelings and circumstances and brought her to places that were more than endless night. She did not like the thick inky smudge of it, which turned the act of creation into a mess. In the home of an overworked single mom, one learns not to be a noise or a mess or a hassle and the smudging made the process all of these things. These were not *the* charcoals but these simple charcoals were a hassle and fright.

Shannon had loved simple forms. She had not been contented with anything so simple as the dancing figures that had failed her but the transformation of geometry into narrative was intriguing. When angles and lines could have lives and feelings and essence, then she could indulge a combination of secrecy and revelation that made her most comfortable. Having been discouraged from making noise, she did not like things to be concrete and resolute. She did not want to reveal herself and yet she longed to be known, to be really known. To be truly known, one must be read and scrutinized, to be seen beyond Dessa, Janelle, Portishead, Mondrian and all the clues left on her dorm wall and known for who she was with fervor, curiosity and deep inquiry.

The darkness became her darkness and she could not abide her darkness. She had been told to smile. She had been told that there were things we just didn't talk about and people we didn't say them to and that we were to keep our secrets close and carry on calmly. The smudges are her fingers, the caw of crows begging to be born. They called out for carrion and there were enough dead and gone that they could be granted it. They smelled the bodies left behind and thirsted for the worms that crawled in them. She did not want to give this up, let it come to the fore and consume her mind, her heart and her hands and then after that, her canvas. It was not right.

But the caws, they were insistent and the dark was thick

and undulating and the smudges were upon her fingers and the charcoals in her hand and they meant something that they wouldn't have meant before. Her father was bleeding on the pavement. His eyes were wide and his mouth was open and he needed the ambulance. Her father was wearing the armor that had not held back the bullet and he was trying to breathe and live to see them again. The crows weren't there that night and yet they circled and yet their beaks were foaming and ravenous and their black, distant eyes aglow with the need for this. GIVEITOUSHUNGRY NO.

They screeched. They shredded. They bore witness to hands on her that did not belong and came down from the sky in a cloud of charcoal black and tore the offender to ribbons. Who had he been? How had it come to pass in the first place? These crows that clamored for birth darkened the skies above these thoughts, cast great black smudges on the moment that hurt. GIVEITTOUSHUNGRYHUNGRYMOREHUNGRY-MORE her fingers were hesitating now.

What would it mean if she let them come to be? They were just shapes, rendered on a canvas. They were just birds like any other birds. Why should it scare her so? Why should it feel like a betrayal to her father bleeding out there, waiting for help after taking the shot that took him away from her? There was more that they hungered for and she knew it and more that she wanted to hold back from feeding them, although they were just birds and shapes upon a canvas, shapes she should not fear as they came from her. She was being ridiculous. She walked away from the canvas, went to the bathroom, washed her hands and let the dark circle the drain. It was gone from her fingers, gone from her mind. Had they left or were they merely sated?

She walked down the hall, head up, mock assertive. She wasn't going to let these weird sensations get the better of her. It was just a fucking charcoal drawing. She knocked on Rem's door three times. Hanging out with Rem would be nice. Unless she wasn't up for it and actually wanted to be alone. She might have actually wanted to be alone but the isolation and the feel of the charcoal on her fingers were fucking with her. The things she was thinking about not thinking of were fucking with her. Rem answered the door. She was grateful that Rem answered the door.

"Hey, bitch."

"Hey, bitch. I was thinking of grabbing a drink at Flanagan's."

Rem's face wrinkled. They hadn't been seeing much of Shannon. Shannon had not been seeing much of anyone. Something had gone down, nothing was said about it, then there was that weird, fucked up lecture and then Shannon was elusive again. Rem had tried to get Shannon to open up and had come to understand that wasn't Shannon's way and that maybe Shannon had wanted to be left alone. It was surprising to see her offering to go out for a drink.

"Yeah, cool. I'll get my coat."

Shannon was greatly relieved. She had missed Rem. She had felt inclined to call but pushed back again and again to the easel and the charcoals and the shadows and the crows that wanted to be born, that wanted to be fed. She had wanted to talk to Rem about the lecture and about what had happened prior to the lecture and what was better off not being said. It was better not being alone right now. It might have been better not being alone at all. Shannon didn't feel like she trusted herself all that much. She kind of wanted to kiss Rem. She really wanted not to think about wanting to kiss Rem.

"Cool."

🪬

FLANAGAN'S WAS DINGY. IT WAS ALWAYS DINGY. THEY could have gone to Grendel's Den but it was pricey and Shannon didn't want to get picked up. She wanted to be out but not to feel like it was a big deal to be out. She wanted company but did not want attention. Flanagan's was good for that. The waitress was in her mid 40s and not going anywhere anytime soon. The middle aged barflies no longer had in them the youthful presumptuousness that would make them think they had a shot in hell. This was not where her classmates were drinking. This too was a selling point.

Shannon ordered a PBR, backed it with a shot of well whiskey. Rem did the same. They silently nursed their beers a bit until they were down low enough to pour the back in. Shannon said nothing more until she gulped down the first swig of boilermaker and let it loosen her up some. It wasn't going to be her last drink but she was happy she was drinking, she felt safe knowing she was drinking.

"I'm glad you're getting out," said Rem.

"Thanks."

Shannon's ears perked up. Someone, something was whispering.

We will peck and shred. We will find it and descend like night upon the Earth. We will rend. We will tear. We will gulp it down then gone. It can be gone. We are waiting. We can smell it. We are hungry. The murder is perched and waiting. We need to be born. We can tear it up and gulp it down and then you can be free of it just listen to us and let us come out and you can be okay and you can say what you need to say and be free of the weight of it all. We have so much to give you and you have so much to feed us if you would just please let us be born.

She did not need to respond. She could tell the voices knew her heart. She zoned out to a far off cawing until Rem brought her back to reality.

"What have you been up to? I see you in class and you're quiet. Are you working on stuff?"

The professor had looked at the work. He was liking the stuff in charcoal, though his eyes kept creeping down her shirt and up her skirt. He keeps on drawing closer and claiming more of her space. She cringes and pushes back, retreats in, stutters some and he tells her that to make it she'll need to be more assertive, which she could be if he wasn't looking at her like that. She apologizes, though she does not know for what. He offers her a chance to work with the Libertine's charcoals. She would like to but can't bring herself to say that. She thanks him and says she wants to do a few more things before handling something so precious. The offer is out there when she's ready. She cringes at the idea of being ready.

"Some stuff in charcoal."

Rem put a hand on their chin.

"Interesting. Yeah. Cool. Maybe something good comes of that shitshow in class."

Shannon smiled.

"Yeah. I like working with them."

They enjoyed a few more drinks. They remembered that they knew and cared for each other again. Shannon let her hand touch Rem's. She could have kissed Rem but didn't know if she wanted to kiss anyone anymore. Maybe not for a while. A hand in hers was nice. A body casually pressed against her. Closeness. Being seen. Being seen was nice. She hadn't thought she was very fond of being seen. Rem was good company. If Rem had asked, she would have gone home with them. It was good that Rem hadn't asked because she definitely wasn't ready for that or what it could mean. Rem and Shannon parted ways.

Too drunk to draw, she lay in bed and felt the judgment and scrutiny of the canvas. She looked in the eyes of Janelle, Dessa, Frida Kahlo and Angela Davis, seeing in them a reminder that she was afraid to be part of anything that mattered that much and she knew guys like Jameson for all their talk didn't want her at the table with anyone who mattered. The crows were cawing, selfish and dismayed. In the morning, it would be finished and they would live.

HOMO FUGE

She did not like being in Jameson's office. She wished that they didn't have to be alone together. She had never cared for his eyes or the feeling of him looming over her. She resented that she needed an advisor to look over her work and make sure she was creating at all. She would rather be left to her peace so that she could just make more of it. Sooner or later, though, she would have to put it in front of someone's eyes and feel the scrutiny of someone understanding her a little deeper and trying to figure out what she was about and where her thoughts and feelings had originated. She had been working a lot with the charcoals and these fears were only amplified. She would be seen and she did not wish to be seen. He was deep in thought or just trying to look like a man who was deep in thought.

At least his eyes were off of her and he wasn't trying to imagine what was under her bulky sweater. At least there was that. But he was looking through the drawings and through them he was seeing that she had done nothing in oils lately and had not felt like rendering any more scenes in oils. He could see now that she had been changed and he had taken part in it and she knew from the men she had in her life that men would take and then take credit. He had told her so and she was all the better for it and now, he no doubt thought that he owned her betterness and was the architect of a new life where she knew what she was now because he had told her that. Did he know this or had he just decided it?

"I like these," he said, indicating the crows, "they're a simple form, heavily shaded. Looks like there's not much going on but the sense of movement and the sense of personality going on here take this to a new level, a lot more than the action in your other pieces. I've always said that I appreciate the sense of movement in your work but it's somehow bigger, more expressive in these charcoals."

He had been precise and political in his praise. He did not hand out too much because otherwise, she would not be hungry for it. He needed her and the others to be hungry for it because then they would get desperate and he needed desperation. She no more wanted to feed him than she wanted to feed those crows. The crows at least offered her the chance to forget. She felt crazy thinking about the crows like that again. They were only a thing she had drawn, just pictures emerging from her own tense, embattled mind. She let her guard down some, feeling self conscious about being so defensive.

"Thank you," she said.

"I mean it," he said, putting a hand on her shoulder, an unwelcome hand but not one she was pushing away. She decided she would trust him for now. She did not decide because she had any such inkling toward him but rather that she desired to trust something, someone, anyone right now.

"I think maybe we should try something."

She now wanted to take his hand off her. She now wanted to flee the office and not come back.

"I don't know," she said.

She didn't like the idea of picking the charcoals back up or of feeling any closer to The Libertine. They had felt wrong in her hand, too insistent and too editorial. The ones she had bought from the art supply store were enough. The feeling that she should buy them in the first place and then from there that she should work with them and the crows that wished to gestate in her mind and on her canvas were enough and she wanted nothing to do with them right now, or rather nothing more.

She was not superstitious or at least she needed not to regard herself as superstitious. She had stopped going to church, even though her mother had begged her to keep going. The church had brought them hot food and comfort after her father's death and she had seen some kindness up until she was old enough to judge. She had let superstition into her world through them and she had been told to trust the god that had made the world that had taken her father from her in the first place. The charcoals were making her superstitious again. She wanted none of it.

"I don't know what you're afraid of," he said, "but whatever it is, the way out is through it. I want you to confront this."

HUNGRY

A shriek somewhere deep in her mind, a shriek that she read as a shriek though there was no sound at all. A sound of desperate, starving, unmitigated and unbridled need. It needed to be born and it needed to eat. It needed her help and promised in return to make the things worth forgetting. There was no knowing why or how this could be or how much say she had in whether or not she would accept the offer but it was there and she wanted to take it. The hands that were on her, the eyes boring holes into her and the sensation of being less than woman, less than person in this man's eyes and measure were too much. She felt the things she covered up were bashing against her brain and longing to come to the fore and that the crows were the only thing that could stop them from doing so.

"I don't know," she said but still took the box when she was offered it. It was an honor. It was a generous offer given to a favored student who was beating the expectations she'd had of herself. She approached the easel in his office and she began to draw, hands guided by the whim of the murder of crows. If this hurt too much then they would go back and shred it, rip its eyes from its sockets, pluck it clean until there was nothing there. If this was trauma, then they'd be fed with trauma. They cawed and called and she answered them stroke by stroke.

Shadowy wings. Shadowy thirsty beaks. Dark, beady eyes that she could see nothing but hunger reflected in. They gained definition and texture from blob to full blown bird now and from bird to full blown murder. The realism was keen but angry and she took them for what she felt them to be in the weird, esoteric place where they made their offer, in the realm that of late, she'd carved out in herself and kept these secrets and this flock of ever-thirsting birds. Her mind drifted for reasons unknown to high school and a group of girls who called her a fucking whore and who had spread rumors about what she'd done with a boy that one of them had liked.

For reasons she did not know, she was back in her room crying and wishing they would leave her alone and that the boys who had called her did not do so full of those expectations. She wished as well that she had not met them, she wished as well that she didn't need to trade what she traded for company and peace and passion and acceptance. She tried not to feel these things freshly and anew as the crows were born but the crows, they cawed for meat and they wanted something raw and they promised they would take that pain from her.

She did not know how it worked as she filled the canvas with that murder of crows but she could sense herself growing calmer, safer somehow. She could sense them swooping down upon those painful moments and pecking apart the resurfaced memories, devouring that trauma that she had fed them and the persecution for which they had hungered so. They were grateful and they were thankful and they were oh-so-pleased to tear and rend and gulp it down in razored beaks. When she was done, she was thinking and drifting no longer, and regarded those pains for once as things of the past. Where once there had been flesh on their bones, they were now ghosts, intangible and incapable of causing her any more suffering.

FEEDUSHUNGRYMORE

Though she felt a freedom she had not felt before drawing, her hands were twitching. There was a closeness she could feel to the professor and to the man whose bones had supposedly been a part of these charcoals. She felt a desire to understand and hear him and, given time, given enough time, maybe, maybe to forgive him. The charcoals were calling out for her hands and her attention and her thoughts and her pain and her vision and her heart and she wanted to think she was just being superstitious and that the crows were just a symbol and the feeling of freedom was only that, a feeling, but she was faced with these odd sensations and did not know what to make of them and she wanted nothing more to do with the charcoals because she wanted so much more to do with the charcoals.

"Thank you," she told him, "these are great."

And they were great, that wasn't a lie. She set the charcoal she was working with down in the box it had come from. She closed her eyes a second to gain composure, to free herself from the idea of hungry crows and unwanted intimacies, from the fear she had of the chalk she had been drawing with. She was ridiculous to think all of this and ridiculous to believe it would have any bearing on who she was or how she lived with what had made her that way. She did not like how much better she felt putting it down or how much better she'd felt with it in her hand.

"You do good work with these. It's repetitive for sure but more and more thorough. I'd like you to stick with these and to try exploring other forms."

If the crows were what the crows felt like, then she did not want to know what other beings she could give birth to or what offers they would present. She thought suddenly of Goya's painting *The Sleep of Reason Produces Monsters* and all the fiends that streamed forth from the discontented soul at the center of it. She did not like what had already been born and the potential of something else, something richer and more complex gave her pause. There would be no explaining this without sounding crazy. There was no feeling this without feeling crazy.

"Thank you," she said, "I will."

"And if you want to try the Libertine's set again, you're worth it."

Again, the hand on shoulder. Again, the body lingering, suspended in her space, might as well be big as a mountain, might as well keep growing. She wouldn't move him from there and he might not move if asked nicely.

"Thank you."

Another stroke of her shoulder. Meaningful eye contact. Perhaps paternalistic, perhaps simply perverse, she couldn't say. She met his eyes and tried not to think about what it would mean if she needed those things to create and if she needed him to grow. She would rather have neither. She left it, she left him. She returned to her canvas, frantically sketching more crows and trying not to see that somewhere on dense black wings, if you squinted, you could see a face.

A NIGHT IN WHITECHAPEL

Shannon was stirred from sleep, awakening and instead of rising, plummeting suddenly into another dream.

Tall and faceless, a shape stood at the foot of her bed wearing a tall hat and cloak. At first she could not see who it was, at first she could not bring herself to move. There was something unreal about this and wrong and she felt she was in a nightmare and could not control her limbs. She felt that it had come to violate her somehow, as some had before but in a way that was deeper and crueler and would last longer. She wanted to flee and yet she had to know what it was that had brought it here and what it was that it had to say to her.

"Soon," it said, "I will have always been with you."

From the canvas, there was the sound of cawing. From the drawings, there was the sound of cawing. The flocks and murders had grown to great proportions. She expected them to rise from the page and consume her but the tall entity with the booming voice had the situation well in hand. The crows were hers and his and they would bring no harm to her, unlike this phantom that clearly had some greater motive. She listened to her cawing and her much louder heartbeat and waited for whatever horrors to play out.

"If you accept me, I can be where you need me," said the ghostly thing. She now had an inkling what it was, who it was that she was speaking to. She begged herself to wake up so she could refuse whatever torments this nightmare was preparing for her. She could hear her heartbeat but odder still, she could feel it and she could feel the chill and the shudder coming through her at this visitor. It reminded her of the offputting and unreal sensation that she had gotten from the charcoals. She knew of course why this was.

She was surprised that she was brave enough to speak up or that words issued from her mouth when she did so. So many times, she had tried to scream when she couldn't bring herself to or tried to cry and found her eyes would not comply.

"Show your face," she said, "I want to know it's you."

She had seen it before, of course. Rendered all in charcoal, unlike the oils for which he had been famous. The face was cold, stern and condescending. There was no joyful superior smirk as one would expect from this man but rather a sense of loss and longing, of an emptiness that would never and could never be filled. He may not have seen this in his face but to her, it was certainly there, frightful as it was, out of place as it was. She had never understood why he had chosen to make his skin pitch black. No art historians had. He had done this one portrait in charcoal and had put his very bones into the ones she used.

"Dante called the dead shades," said Kemp, the Libertine, "I have always been as much dead as alive. Now I am as alive as I am dead. Shadow as much as solid. Ash. You can come with me and we can talk. Find me and we can talk."

The wall opened and he walked through and he was gone, out into somewhere else. She could have been relieved, should have been relieved that he had gone but this was not so. She could find in her the strength to rise and when she found it, she felt that it was best to do so and so she did. She rose and she followed in the path of the ghost that had gone, through a space behind the wall and out into the cruelty and chaos of the old and unknown night.

She followed the figure through paintings of contorted

London streets, past toothless, deformed and pockmarked beggars, past corpulent aristocrats groping prostitutes with thirsty, vampiric faces, sharp and foreign, xenophobic and undeserving of trust. She was in another's London and needed to catch up with him. She could have and perhaps should have told herself that this man was a harbinger of something dreadful and had made his world with scorn and lured her into it but this was a dream and she was certain only of the needs built into the walls of the dream instead of the needs of her heart and soul and conscience.

The backdrop was a bluegrey, muted and wrong. She knew this place, this painting, where it was night inside the building somehow and daybreak would never come to this pub. The subhuman bucktoothed patrons raised glasses in the air and never consumed the overly foamy beer inside them. The cleavage of a sad, zaftig waitress spilled out into her face, dimpled and exaggerated. This was the rich man's burlesque of poverty, presented now in oils and wrapped around her. Why was this man who had so little in common with her even bothering to reach out? He saw her world as contemptible, subhuman and deserving only of the most derisive and condescending of treatments.

His work's perception of a black face was as condescending as any minstrel show's but somehow more mean-spirited. It was rougher and rounder, covered in stylized bumps and creases that portrayed more than hard work and careworn laughter. It was the kind of thing which led him to be regarded as a product of his time. This wasn't something she bought because she was at a loss to imagine a time that these thoughts wouldn't be a product of. She did not feel optimistic that there ever would be such a time. There was something in that face that revealed how they were not alike and never could be. He hated her as he hated all other people.

"I don't think you look like that," said Kemp, his charcoaled face unmoving and still a mask of despite, "you are quite beautiful."

"You don't believe in beauty," Shannon shot back. She

wanted to get out of there and to be free of him. She wanted to wake up and find him gone forever from her and to never again lay hands on those charcoals that had brought him closer to her. Whatever this was was not a dream, not entirely.

"And you do believe in beauty? I can feel it in you. Nothing beautiful or kind has ever happened for you. Nothing kind or beautiful unless you make it. You can make it. You can be freed from those who took that from you and you can find what I couldn't from life. If you do the work."

She didn't like the sound of it.

"The work? Your work ruined people. You made a woman burn her face, tortured another for months. You were a fucking monster who thought your work mattered more than other people."

Though his face did not move, his body was seething, shaking. The charcoal face could not shift its expression, yet he struggled to remain seated, he struggled not to scream or snarl. This thing she was talking to was unstable and not to be trifled with. She told herself this because she wasn't going to be part of it, whatever it was.

" I ruined nobody. I revealed them. The face beneath is the true one. We must pursue the face beneath."

"I don't know what the fuck you mean."

"You do. You will."

SHE WOKE UP BACK IN THE ART ROOM. IT WAS A DREAM IN A dream. She had some strange neurotic terror of touching the charcoals and because she had she felt guilt and that she had validated Kemp and all of his bullshit; the racism, the nihilism, the abuse. She had said to the world in her decision to work with the charcoals that Kemp was worthwhile and worth connecting with and understanding. She had said in her choice to work with the charcoals that his was a legacy that mattered and could be approached and worked with. She was disturbed by the dream but further disturbed that she wanted to go to the canvas and create more, and to work again with the charcoals. She had psyched herself out, combined her recent unresolved trauma with her feeling that the professor was weird with her and had mystified the experience of working with these things.

She did not feel well rested. She did not feel much like she had had a nightmare. She may have been dreaming but maybe this was something else. She walked to the canvas and with shaking hands she started to draw and hoped the drawing would rid her of these feelings.

"Can I take these home?" she asked, as the halfhearted scribble concluded. If it could accost her for making it incomplete, it would have risen from the canvas and shaken her until granted limbs and heart and structural integrity. It wasn't like the crows though, there was no force of animation. She was thinking instead about how much she needed the charcoals and what she could do with them when she had some time alone with them.

"I don't think I can do that," the professor said, "but I've got some work to do and you can hang here and draw while I do it. Might be nice to have the company."

"I really need more time with these. There's something special about working with them. You're right. You can feel the history."

He shrugged.

"I can't deny that, but no."

He placed the charcoals in their box. She did not even notice herself reaching out for that box as he placed it back in the desk drawer. Out of her sight but not out of her mind. Buried, away from her. It felt too far away, its promises would die on the vine, its art would go unmade by her, the connection would go unforged and while she had fought it and while she had thought it was the last thing she wanted and in those dream streets, she had all but spat on the Libertine's face, that wasn't what was happening now and that wasn't what she longed for and what she needed now. It was denied her as quickly as it had been offered. This was his way. She had previously resented it but she had other, deeper concerns.

"I need it," she said. The words weren't words, they were howls of the starved. They were spoken in the hungerspeech with which methheads asked for change and cats yowled for their dinner, that universal language of can't-live-without that predators hear as only "I came to trade". And from "I came to trade", he tried not to light his eyes up and illuminate his purpose and tried not to make the offer before she made it. He shook his head, negotiating fiercely and letting the next repetition bounce right off him.

"It was stipulated in the donation that they be used but still that doesn't mean I don't have to be careful with them. You can work with them here while I supervise but if I let you bring them home too often, then something could happen and if something happens, it could cost me my job."

She did not argue with this. She had said that she'd come here to trade and knew she'd said it. She unbuttoned the first button of her blouse, she came closer and made clear with her eyes the exchange that was to be made. He took the second button and undid it for himself not knowing the crows already flying around her mind, not knowing the memory made was another one to be ripped up and slurped down and rendered inert so it wouldn't come back to harm her. He may have cared. It may have chilled and saddened him to think why she did this and how it made her feel but he took what he was offered, bent over the desk and fading into the inky cloud of trauma eating birds. She would look back and find this a movie she saw and remember nothing of his touch, then turn around and look back and find nothing at all.

❦

SHE CAME HOME VICTORIOUS AFTER A FASHION. SHE HAD the priceless relic in her hands, calling to her the whole way to the dorm, pleading with her to let what was in gestation finally be born and in birth do what had to be done. She let the charcoals out of the box and with shaking hands she went to the easel. She let the crows digest what had just happened and she closed her eyes and begged the voices that were not hers to be silent so she could decide, whatever it was she was deciding. She could put down the charcoals and walk away from the easel. She could pick up the paints and she could let the dancing shapes be born again even if all they had to offer were lies.

The cawing ceased. The seductive whispers from the charcoal faded out a moment. She closed her eyes and saw the face again, the Libertine. He had offered her freedom from feeling like this. The crows were a gift she saw now and what they gave was nothing compared to what the charcoals offered and what the Libertine presented. In life, he had been a monster and that made her hesitant but the charcoals felt right in her hands and the crows made her life so much easier to live. The power, the violence, the raw opacity of everything that had haunted her had been ripped up in hungry beaks and freedom was close at hand.

In fevered strokes, she made the choice as she had made the choice to let crows be born and to feast on that which held her back. In measured lines she reaffirmed the promise, slowing down and giving the cause precision. In the dedicated and methodical and the mad and the frenzied, she said "yes" again to freedom and to the chance to be unafraid or just to fear only herself. She had always felt in the works of white bullshit canon that it was a great luxury to fear only oneself and those who did so tossed around bricks of privilege.

Yes, she said to the shape that asserted its way from imagination to mind's eye to canvas, even if she was at the same time repulsed and even if she had no respect for the monster. Respect is in the terms for few surrenders. The Libertine was dead besides. The worst he'd done had happened and now he could do it for her. She told herself again and again that this was not a betrayal and she'd still be who she was before committing the charcoals to the task. She told herself she wasn't lying to herself and not to worry. She told herself she need not ask herself her own permission. Too many thoughts that weren't of the task at hand, too many thoughts.

She let the face emerge fully formed. She backed away and reached for the phone, thinking to call Rem or to go get herself a joint or a drink. Like the dream it was realer than it had ever needed to be. She was frightened and yet relieved to see it so real. The realer it was, the less crazy she was and that was something. But then, if she weren't crazy, then all of this was too real. The charcoal face of Thomas Kemp was born upon that canvas and now those eyes were looking on her expectantly. She could tear the canvas and bring back the charcoals and this would get no deeper.

"You're not there," she told the face, which gave no response. She had decided it could exist and thus decided she could choose for it not to. The face of Thomas Kemp did not argue. It was a drawing she'd made. Still, she walked closer to the canvas, reminding herself that it was only a picture she'd drawn and that she was just falling prey to anxiety, though her anxiety of late had been somewhat better. It wasn't because of the crows. That made no sense.

"You're not there," she repeated, trying her hardest to plant her feet in a world where he was not. There was more than enough in this life that didn't make sense. He wasn't there. He couldn't be there, a morsel of half digested trauma, more stress than ghost for certain. There are no ghosts. If there were ghosts SHUT UP NOT NOW there are no ghosts...

Still, she walked up to the canvas and still she reached out and still somehow her hands could pull the face out from the canvas. Somehow she now had it in her hand. The dark, judgmental face of Thomas Kemp now rested in her hands. She could toss it in the trash if she wanted. Stll, somehow, she pressed it on her own and then, somehow it seeped beneath her skin. The canvas was blank and now she wore the face beneath.

THE PASSION OF SAINT JOAN

T he second panel of the triptych depicts a woman's battered weeping face, almost aglow with suffering. Her eyes are looking upward in a perfect and sublime moment of betrayal and horror. It is called *The Passion of Saint Joan.*

THEY'RE GOING TO FUCK US

S hannon dreamed of the closeness of Thomas Kemp, of the face she pulled from the canvas and put beneath her own to cement their connection. He led her to the spot where she was needed. She was standing at the scene -- the one scene, the first disappointment and the first proof that life was not going to be kind to her even if she was good and quiet and patient. She watched her father bleed out, trembling and struggling and hoping she'd wake. Instead, she called over the crows and with their hungry beaks, they descended. The moment it started, it was wrong.

Those beaks, those talons dug in, their beady eyes all the while focused on the one who had brought them, trying to express something that was akin to gratitude but not altogether that thing. As they tore strings of him, shredded bits of eyeball gelatin and ripped the face from him until he was no longer recognizable, just blood and tears and a big mass of black that grew and gathered and called other crows, murders and murders from somewhere else until at last there was nothing of the scene but the cloud of black feathers that devoured the dream.

She awakened, finding Kemp there. She closed her eyes and breathed and focused. She didn't want to look at him yet or to find that he was actually there. They had become too much connected already and she hoped that she would be able to deny this or banish it with reason. Or maybe if she ignored him then he would go away back to hell or history or the muddied well of her subconscious. She could be alone, she was sure and she could move on and return the charcoals. She could fess up or switch them back if she needed to. Unless she couldn't.

The cawing and the blank tyrant canvas pulled her from her attempt to find some peace. She went to the canvas, charcoals in hand, wondering what life tried to assert itself into being. She had given life to the crows already, so she knew that the things in her hand had power and what she created truly mattered. She shooed the crows, feeling a need to see clearly, to perceive even the pain they would have devoured. She may have feared what she would create but she had to see it on her terms.

She delved deep, seeking the places where the crows were at their most ravenous and where their heavy wings would have the most to hide. She should have known where this would take her. Her mother could have told her, a therapist could have told her. For all that she kept quiet about, Rem could have told her. She had grown a thick skin when it regarded the insults, the casual racism, the harassment and the isolation. She had come to terms more or less with the loss of inhibitions and the stupid men that pain had led her into the arms of. She had gotten to the point where she could no longer count or regret missed opportunities.

She had never seen the place where the body fell but she had dreamed of it at times, provided details by overheard conversations between her mother and various aunts and uncles. She imagined it with the greatest of acuity her whole life, trying to push the thoughts of it back. Kemp had said that soon he would have always been with her. She hoped that this was not what he had meant. She curled her lip at the thought that she had lived so long with the gifts of a monster. And yet, she had always seen this as clearly as if it had been right in front of her eyes.

On the pavement at the moment of his demise, Brandon Hernandez looked right at his daughter, pleading wordlessly for her to help him. The bullet wound was oozing and the bullet wound would stay. A few feet away, his killer was dead and help would only come in the form of a young woman with a set of charcoals made from a monster's bones. Help had still come too late.

It would not come in time to mend a defective vest or calm the rage of the meth head from Southie that needed those forty bucks in the till every bit as much as Brandon needed to go home and see his wife and daughter, every bit as much as the man needed to live. Moreso maybe but she didn't want to feel that for him. She wanted her father back and didn't mind if this guy bled out as he had in life and her dad came back safe.

"I need you to know this," he'd once said, glassy eyed, distant someplace else after a shit day of being a cop in Southie, "people are generally good, kid but I'll tell you, when it comes to rich folks, when it comes to white folks, sooner or later, they're gonna fuck us. In the end, they always fuck us."

She focused on this moment and let the charcoals and her hands usher him back. She recreated that face full of pleading and betrayal, the hole in his chest that had saved the department a few hundred dollars that they ended up paying out anyway as death benefits. She recreated the hand reaching out for anyone, even the man who had shot him down and been wounded by him but right now wanted most of all for his daughter to help him stand up.

The crows cawed loud and tried to swarm but she would not have them right now, even as she felt the sting of never being able to help and the guilt from how hard she tried to forget and how much the crows had gorged upon these feelings on their way up to the forefront of her thoughts.

"Shut up!" she shouted, sketching furious textures, grinding the fatal pool of blood into the canvas. They parted, croaking quietly now but certainly still protesting. She took Kemp's gift and watched from this place as the system he had given everything to now took the last thing he had left, as he had promised it and as it had promised him. Her mother had said he died a hero and he was surely proud of having given all he had. She had tried to tell herself that her mother had to be right and that it made things a little bit better. Rather, she had told herself that that made things better. She could see from the moment that she was wrong.

She jumped as she heard breaths from the canvas. Laboring breaths, coughing, choking, moaning. Nothing in this seemed heroic, nothing in this seemed right. She struggled to let herself be pleased with what she'd done and the impact it created. Like rope, like net, like seaweed on her ankles, she battled to be free of the feeling that she was not saving him but killing him again or that she was complicit in abomination, giving the force of animation to this man who had sacrificed his life doing what he'd sworn to and upholding what he'd felt was the peace of the public.

The charcoal hand reached out, unbound by life in canvas, unbound by the line between reality and fabrication. Unbound by time and a recalled bulletproof vest. She could have fled the room and gone to drink until the crows could flocktogether and eat all of this and she would be done with whatever was going on here now. She knew she could call on Kemp but worried that he would only spur her on to the worst. This was her father though, even if it was the memory of a cop dying on the pavement brought to life by his daughter with a medium she no longer trusted.

She took his hand and pulled and dragged and with all her might, she took him from death and conceit and into life. The bleeding corpse emerged, slumping to the floor, hand on the wound, trying to keep in the black congealed pool of guts and to maintain the little link he had to life. He could just die here again on the floor and she would lose him again, so he went to her knees, placing her own hands over the wound, pressing on it.

"Please don't go again," she begged him.

His eyes were still a dying man's eyes. His face was still agape with fear and disappointment, still locked in the silent, primal banshee shriek. He may have been an image from the past but he was all too real and all too vulnerable and all too likely to fade. She pressed down, the black blood that she had drawn herself soaking her hands. She sobbed, begging for him to live.

"Please, please don't go again," she said, "I'm so afraid. I'm so alone. I needed you and you left me all alone with a woman who couldn't cope with me. Stay with me."

The simulacrum, eternally frightened, had no words of love or of consolation. He said nothing to try and bring peace or pleasure to his daughter. He said only one phrase and it was one that rang deep and true but nonetheless did not bring consolation. It reminded her that he bled out on the street, killed by a cheap and shoddy vest and a partner that didn't care to risk his life again.

"They're gonna fuck us," he said, heavy with sorrow, drooling dark blood, "in the end, they always fuck us."

She knew he wasn't wrong.

AUDIENCE

W hen Branwell returned from a trip across Europe to fawn over the grotesqueries Kemp had painted, Kemp should have been suspicious but for some reason, he felt compelled to hand to Branwell some paintings to show this mysterious Duke. Then, uncharacteristically, Kemp surrendered to Branwell's suggestion that he go out to the Duke's home and meet this patron who had taken an interest in him and had come to the Duke's manor. Met at the door by a nervous maid with prominent bruises on what was clearly a face chosen for its delicacy, Kemp set aside his thoughts of what he had done to his own lover to seriously regard the man as some sort of brute. He did not think much of the working class but had found no joy in the aristocracy's fondness for humiliating and mistreating them. He was thus quite sure that he would not regard this man fondly when he met him.

Awe still came to meet Kemp. Fear as well but mostly at the sight of the gentleman towering above him in his tall hat and blood red longcoat, he felt awe. The Duke was middle-aged and at the apex of all that one would call distinguished, with a proud Roman nose, severe steel grey eyes, a powerful jaw and an immaculately trimmed mustache; he was a vision of

GARRETT COOK

authority and machismo. Though at least twenty years his senior and several more by reputation, Kemp was certain this man was twice as strong as he and the survivor of exploits he would never have thought to attempt. The Duke was the very essence of everything the rich and worthless friends that he had cultivated pretended that they were.

"It is a pleasure to meet you, Mister Kemp," said the Duke in a powerful baritone. "Your work is not exhibited often but where it has been, so too have I been. It is a travesty that your art is not better known but it is my belief that I can assist you with that and make arrangements that are to the benefit of us both."

This man who had impressed Kemp so did not mince words about his intentions. He had been powerful and direct in his choices. Kemp might have thought he was unsure of whether he deserved such acclaim but if he thought about it for any length of time, he was sure that he wasn't. He wasn't going to say it but something about this man, simultaneously lean and powerful, dignified and savage, said that he would know.

"There aren't many, sir, who appreciate my art," said a humbled Kemp, a man who none would have recognized, "but I thank you for your kind words. They don't come often."

The Duke laughed and placed a large hand on Kemp's shoulder. The gesture made him no less nervous.

"Yes, I suppose they don't. I have seen your work and I can tell from Branwell and just seeing you now that you are an acquired taste, Mr. Kemp. If I were you I wouldn't worry about it, though. I have often worked with men like yourself. The work and the man are challenging. Neither connect so easily with the eyes, the ears, the stomach. You know why that is?"

Kemp shook his head as the Duke led him past several hallways full of doors. There were screams and cries of ecstasy coming from behind some of them. Kemp's head craned to listen, his hands longed to crack them open and see inside. Whatever was occurring in there frightened him but unlike most things, they did not bore or alienate him. In the presence of the Duke, in the presence of this mayhem, Kemp experienced a sensation that had long eluded him: that of curiosity. Perhaps his art had often suffered for it. Through cracked open doors, he could see bodies writhing together and pale, bared flesh struck by whips or chains, or marred by the flames of a candle.

He was surprised when they settled in a study very like his own, though more opulently appointed, with pages torn from old, weird manuscripts. There were images of naked men with horse heads, hippopotami with lion bodies, a strange king on the back of a humanoid camel, wheels of limbs, squat dwarves holding onto pronounced and spiny erections. Dismayed faces of cruel nobles gloated from inside the frames. Kemp instantly hated these people in the paintings and understood them to be the inner selves of the aristocrats he'd grown to hate.

A maid came in bearing a tray balancing a bottle of absinthe, two glasses and a small naptha torch, heating up the liquor and melting sugar cubes into it. She stood and waited for them to drink, ready to prepare more. The Duke took up one of the glasses.

"Drink with me," he said and Kemp did as he was told immediately. There was nothing about The Duke that he could say no to, even if fear, surprise, and curiosity were grinding on his mind.

"It's lovely," said Kemp, though he was neither fond of the bitterness of anise or of the courtesy of lying to protect another's feelings. If he were to put the glass down, there would be consequences whatever they might be.

"It's not," said the Duke, "but it will be, Kemp. It will be perfection. Do you believe me?"

Kemp kept his head down, now wishing he had not chosen to come or that he could escape now that he had. The impulse to flee was strong, even as his mind started to cloud.

"No," said Kemp, "I don't believe you at all. I think you're testing me for some reason."

"Perceptive," said the Duke.

The room turned round, spun like a clock. The world slanted vertical, straightened up, then rolled over and turned once again. Kemp held the chair for dear life. This was not simple absinthe. There were other forces at work here. He could swear that one of the pages on the wall depicted the Duke, a man with large wings astride a giant leonine, bullish beast that also bore the face of a man. Back and forth he looked and saw that these two surely were no different. It was odd. The aspect on the page had not looked much like the Duke before but now the faces were trading back and forth.

"Claim it and claim the face beneath," said the Duke, "you will have the legacy. The legacy will have you. It is in your bones, Thomas Kemp. The tradition is long and proud."

A rotund naked man held up a large dog, taking enthusiastic chomps from the animal's cadaver, pulling out entrails, sinew and fur all at once with the same zealous hunger. There was something familiar in this man's countenance as well, not from the pages of the book but from the Renaissance self portrait on the opposite wall, a man who had been considered the equal of Raphael but had the reputation of Cellini. There had been whispers of other proclivities but those were not important as this man was a man deceased for over three hundred years as far as Kemp had known. This wasn't right. This was whatever he drank. He got up on teetering legs, walking through the tilted hallways full of screams, occasionally seeing the gluttonous painter, dead dog in his arms just ahead.

Sounds of whips and chains. Sounds of orgasmic joy. Sounds of weeping. Endless chomping of the dog's body. He watched the glutton who he had thought he'd left behind him vomit heaving chunks of dog upon the floor then crawl on his knees to consume it again, all the while bearing a gaping smile and a knowing look. Would he die here? Would it be forever before he reached the door? So many hallways, more than this building could have contained. Out of the corner of his eye, a robed figure appeared with what looked like his own pistol on a cushion. He reached out for it but then dismissed it as a hallucination.

Through this all too massive mansion Kemp ran, expecting no end but still resolute in escaping. The dogeater close behind him mockingly brayed like a donkey. From the rooms, the orgasm screams now intermingled with the sounds of gunshot and the voice of his father reprimanding him. He stopped and listened to the calls of "deviant", "failure", "disgrace" and "monster." The sounds of his father having his way with the chambermaid. The sounds of his mother dying of consumption. The sounds of the maid being beaten into silence. A naked phantom ran down the hall, trailing behind him, begging for his assistance. He did not look back to see who it was. He knew already.

Again, the robed creature offered the pillow but he stopped himself from reaching out. With all his strength of will, with all that was in his mind and body and his wounded heart, he dashed for the door, which he expected to remain locked or obstructed. Perhaps he expected something to interpose itself between him and the exit but no such thing occurred.

๛

KEMP AWAKENED, MIND ON FIRE, EYES BLURRED. HE WAS back in his study, an empty decanter of brandy on his desk, an unfinished painting from his studio posed to tease him. He looked it over and saw that it revealed no more about the crowds than his last ones had, and he had, if anything, grown more estranged and less sure about human nature. He had the approval and support of a woman who loved him and the one friend he had left in the world but this had been insufficient. The unclear visages of pubgoers wanted some semblance of soul but they would never get it from him.

He had seen such bizarre figures as the absinthe and cryptic talk had blackjacked him at the Duke's house. He could not be sure how much of what he remembered was real or how much of it he could act upon or feel comfortable looking at again. He could not even be sure of whether the Duke was anything like he remembered him or he had simply been drawn into the man's mystique. He would not have been the first. Branwell had, after all, spoken upon the Duke as a wonder of the world and a great mystery of life, instead of simply a wealthy deviant with a big house full of expensive liquor and perverse hangers-on. He could see what he had seen in the Duke but hoped for the sake of Branwell's mind and soul that there were also some things he had not.

The first knock upon the door of the study was breakfast. He did not thank Sybil for it and she did not make any inquiries about how the night had gone. He imagined she simply wanted to hasten herself to Branwell's bed, which was just as well because he could not imagine touching anyone today and felt somehow disconnected from this woman who had given so much to him. There was a tinge of guilt and one of disgust. The drawer and the pistol were calling.

He took out the weapon and tried to banish from his thoughts the entertainments provided by the Duke's retinue, the spinning cruelties and the aura of unrepentant wrongs. The bullet would blow them out, along with every semblance of that which was Thomas Kemp. It was not right to be Thomas Kemp, and all the sad faces and dire admonitions about this were correct. He'd been offered some sort of patronage by someone that did not feel human and someone who might have no longer seen him as human either. This wouldn't be altogether wrong.

The incomplete faces of tradesmen and barmaids that he'd never know, the latest of those particular redundancies were not born yet but he could see in the lines he'd started a pity and contempt. Theirs was not the only ugliness. Kemp could do nothing about theirs but could liberate the world from his own, if he only squeezed that trigger that had so often seduced him but could never finish the act.

Pity. It had always been a pity. Though he had created what Branwell and Sybil had said were magnificent paintings, he had never connected with the subjects and he had shown nothing so much as his disgust. If on their faces, there had been this same disgust, and in the voices of the fops he'd thought himself above there had been such disgust, then he was no wiser or greater than they and his fears that he had little to give but hypocrisy must have been well founded. If he could only squeeze that trigger, then the world would be a little less ugly.

He returned the pistol to its place, hung his head and cried. He could not squeeze that trigger, not at his bravest, no. He may not have valued life but he clung to it tightly, not knowing what was to be had from it but afraid of whatever it felt like to be without it. He'd had enough of quiet and isolation and he did not much fancy doing anything forever, especially nothing but sleep or suffer. There would be no amount of hatred for himself or the world that would fix that. He cried there, turning feelings he could not make sense of into sobs and screams until he was roused from this by the second knock.

He almost did not answer the door until the weight of being alone with the heaviness of this newfound shock and horror got to him and he welcomed company, letting Branwell in to sit down without any greetings or questions or jibes. He let Branwell sit because Branwell was not the Duke or the pistol or a world whose frightfulness was not the product of his sensitivities and prejudices but rather its own toxic and corroded nature. There had been a time when he would have taken much sadistic delight in feeling that he could depict the world as it was or that the faces beneath people's faces were rotten and monstrous and nothing like what men would like to call human.

"You saw some things," said Branwell, "that you can't understand. I am sorry that I couldn't prepare you, Thomas. For all of your hardness and your airs, you are as fragile as you are powerful. Know, my friend, that I love you as a brother and he needed you to bear witness. You must bear witness to truly make the choice."

Kemp now saw purpose in the pistol. He withdrew it from

the drawer and pointed it at Branwell, eyes still wet and hands still threatening to betray him and drop the weapon.

"I trusted you and you brought me to hell. I did not know there was a hell but now you've called me there and I've felt it and I'm changed forever. I was going to shoot myself with this thing."

Branwell laughed, a strange, animalistic laugh. His whole face opened into it and those explosions of laughter burst forth. He shook his head in smug disbelief.

"Whatever for, Thomas? You finally get to really see everything. You were sharp, insightful even, and gifted at showing that to others but there was so much you weren't ready for yet and now, Thomas, you are. Killing yourself when you're at your most alive is the most preposterous thing I've heard. I gave you a gift. You should use it."

"I hate your gift, Branwell, and now I hate you."

Branwell's grin returned.

"Then by all means, Thomas, I think all that can be done is for you to pull that trigger."

Kemp observed his former friend and the hideous, mocking smile and he could not find a reason not to do as he said, at least in that moment, he could find no reason. While Thomas Kemp had observed people with contempt and condescension and thought that the world would be better off without many of them, he had not been taken much with violence. He had walked about wishing harm upon most everyone he saw but seldom had he endeavoured to inflict it. He pulled the trigger and changed this, sending a shot into the chest of a once loving friend.

There was a spray of blood as Branwell fell back, the chair tumbling over on top of him. He was bleeding profusely now, he was pinned under the armchair and still he had that expectant smile on his face.

"I'm going to die here, Thomas. You've killed me."

Kemp turned away from his friend, breathing heavily. Branwell was right. He had murdered a man and he would not be able to walk away from the consequences. Branwell was wealthy and connected and had friends, some of whom were very wealthy and dangerous. One of whom he swore he could feel watching him right now, in spite of the impossibility of it all. Branwell's last words revealed how foolish he had been thinking his friend such a simple and parochial mind. He had underestimated the depth of both his passions and his contempt for life.

The mere thought had been enough to make the Duke appear right beside him, wearing an expression that perhaps Branwell had been trying to ape, an expression that would have forced him to point the pistol at a flesh-and-blood man, which he was now certain the Duke was not. He was certain now that the Duke represented something harsh, ancient and unnameable and was more that than he was anything else. He now understood the vision of the tapestry and that he stood before someone whose authority extended beyond his ken.

"You have thought yourself free, Kemp, with all your money and your vicious paintings. You have believed that your despair was a failure on the part of an Earth with nothing to offer. And now, facing punishment for the murder of your only true friend, you see that you have never tasted freedom."

Stepping from seemingly nowhere, the Glutton appeared, hunched down and placing his head affectionately against the Duke's thigh.

"This beast was a great Renaissance painter. Had a taste for children though. Smothered one of his precious cherubim and I was there to help and to offer him an understanding of his hungers. A skinny thing he was, until he decided to make use of the urchins he painted in every possible way. I made a paint brush from one of those overeager fingerbones. I made the bristles from his pubic hair and he continues to inspire and delight. Isn't he delightful?"

Kemp shook his head, mortified.

"He's a monster. You took a deviant and turned him into an ogre."

The Glutton crawled to the body of Branwell, sinking teeth into the man's throat, ripping out large chunks and making big loud, dramatic swallows, stroking his cock all the while. Kemp closed his eyes but found himself still looking at the same scene. So he watched the manbeast consuming great globs of his friend, faster and faster. Time was standing still but the Glutton was speeding up, crunching, slurping, swallowing and utterly devouring the corpse on the floor.

"You will owe this ogre your freedom. He will leave none of the body behind."

Kemp stifled the urge to retch.

"And what will I owe you?"

The Duke shrugged, settling into Kemp's chair.

"You will find the price acceptable and your options are not numerous. My generosity is beyond compare. There is so much to see and know and do, Mr. Kemp. Signor Argenti is not the only one in my retinue, nor the only one with gifts to offer. Brother Gustav," said the Duke, "is the author of many notable texts, illuminated and illustrated with great dedication. He was not a man prone to excess, Brother Gustav, but one whose texts spread concepts and wisdom that no man should experience and none should act upon. I gave him such visions and he was generous with them, as generous as he was with his very flesh."

"I know of the books," Kemp said with a heavy swallow. He'd been told of them before, the extravagance and the unearthly imagery. He had attempted to acquire some of these particular relics at auction but had been outbid by men whose depravity and resources ran deeper than his, who might have deserved the Duke's attention more than he did.

The Duke reclined, the cushion of the chair sinking down deep as he did so, as if he and the furniture were one.

"If you'd like, then you could read them. I can have him bring them to you. I'll need you to do the commission. I need you, Thomas, to be the artist you're supposed to become. Your work is too important to die on the vine because you hold yourself back or finally get the balls to put that pistol to your head and finish yourself. Do you want to read the books?"

For all of his claims, Kemp's commitments even to cruelty

were flimsy. Much of his rage and caprice was a product of boredom and alienation and less of it was wrought from true malice. To read these books would be a commitment to wickedness, an idea he entertained in conversation but one that was not as much a part of his psyche as he would have his acquaintances, particularly his foils, believe.

"That won't be necessary," said Kemp.

"And yet you should know," said the Duke languidly.

Suddenly, the room began to feel cold and damp. There was a stench in the air, one of rot and dust and books falling apart. Then, from some pocket of nothing, a shape appeared in the room, a figure in tattered grey robes, with pulsating bared muscles and sinews for a face. Blood and tissue clung idly to an open sore of a head. It held close to itself an illuminated manuscript whose cover was surely made from the cured skin of some unfortunate novice.

"Was flesh, now canvas," the monk declared, hissing through a raw and bloodied mouth.

Kemp wished to retch or flee and yet did neither. He had fallen to sloth before in the presence of the gun and fell to terror now in the presence of this phantom. He regretted his drinks with the Duke and his words on the nature of virtue, whether he had believed them or not and whether he truly separated art and virtue as much as he claimed to do. He sat and he waited, knowing he was at the mercy of someone who was not just a patron of the arts but a patron of something bigger than he could comprehend.

"Who are you?" Kemp asked, longing to back off and flee the room and to forget.

"I am a patron and the bearer of a legacy that can be yours. You are not a religious man so would scarce understand my place in the hierarchies of Hell. I am a giver of greatness, a greatness which could be yours if you set yourself free to seize it. Your art and your potential are worth it, Mr. Kemp. The price that must be paid is worth it."

Centuries ahead, Kemp would regret this moment of frailty and regret letting the Duke into his heart. He would regret seizing the skin canvas he was offered so that he could paint his true masterpieces. Though he had briefly thought it better to die than to live in a world where beings like the Duke trafficked in the bodies of the wicked and handed down sins as an inheritance, Kemp nodded and took what he was given and all that it meant.

HANDS

"There are urban legends surrounding Cresci," Jameson told the class as the slide deck reached a painting of three cherubim on a cloud, their mouths wide open in agony, "that the fear in the eyes of these angels was a confession of pedophilic tendencies. You look at these angels and the suffering of the innocents and you do see children in intense pain."

Shannon shook in her seat. The crows thirsted for her recognition. So much surging up as she looked into those eyes. She could find in those exquisitely detailed children something that she had seen and experienced herself, the moments of stolen innocence. She wanted to ask them what he had done to them and somehow she felt as if they might answer. She did not have to speculate very hard.

"One of ours," came the whispered voice of Thomas Kemp. She heard the yelp of a dog. The smacking of lips. The crunch of bone. She believed him but did not want to ask any further. The crows pecked at the disgust that rose up from her, from recognition, from outrage. She settled into her chair, her spine no longer stiff and straight as a board. She caught faint echoes of the conversations back and forth, of the disgust of her classmates and of Jameson's defenses. The smacking of lips. The crunch of bone. The whimper of a dying dog.

Background chatter, whispers went thundering loud. Every text notification that someone had forgotten to mute was the shell of a cannon. Footsteps in the hall were shuffling arms, distant sirens close enough that they were driving through the wall, getting out and making ready to punish for the myriad existential crimes on the rap sheet that was being Shannon. They knew what she had done, what she was planning and who she was in league with. If he was the devil, if the charcoal was the devil then they knew she'd chosen the devil.

She twitched and suffered through class. She held her comments, barely knowing what she would have to say if she were listening. Who cared anyway? Who wanted to hear from her? She was gross and sold out to something shitty, ready to remake the pact again and again. There was something she was trying to remember and it bothered her that she was trying to recall it but the crows were merciful, the crows needed her to feel safe.

"We will go if you let him take back the charcoal. We are not numerous enough to keep you safe. We cannot do it alone."

She nodded mutely as if simply showing she was following the lecture. She was shuddering at the thought of a future where she could remember. No, she needed this. She needed the distance. Whatever she did, there would be a means to forget and be safe.

🐦

SHE WENT BACK TO JAMESON'S OFFICE WHILE THE OTHERS moved on. He looked over the growing output, pouring out platitudes that made her uncomfortable, laying hands on her and it made her uncomfortable but the crows were there, swarming and waiting, hungry for the disquiet, hungry for the experience, eager to let her back into it and drift away so that this could vanish into their greedy guts. She focused on the Dick Blick charcoals in her purse, waiting for the chance to make the substitution she needed. She had supposedly come to return them.

Jameson poured two shots.

"You'll have a drink with me, won't you?"

She smiled. Playing the femme fatale. Playing him. This was going to be worth it. She needed what he had, she needed what he could give her even if she fucking hated needing it. She was good enough without him. She had enough vision without him. She had been chosen for this instead of him and yet, here she was, having to give in like this and do shots with her professor to get the things she needed. Fucking disgusting.

A PIERCING CAW. A BURST OF FEATHERS. A WORLD TORN UP and gouged and eaten. Borne away from herself, she could sit back and wait and say what he needed to hear, do what he needed done until he left the room and she could make the switch. The charcoals needed her and she needed them, the crows, the whispered advice, the influx of all things new and vibrant and possible came from this terrible bargain she was making. She saw through her eyes only as she took the ashen artifacts and traded them away, exalting a moment in all that would be born.

Whatever she was giving, whatever she needed to forget, he was thinking small. Goddammit. He was thinking small. How fucked up was that? She couldn't see or remember much of anything until she was back at home at the easel, inexplicably feeling like weeping, trying to avoid the aftershock of ghostly fingers all over her body from the trade she had made for these things. She hyperventilated and laughed intermittently as she began to sketch a set of hands, dark and strong and given life by the conviction behind her strokes.

Soon, they were on her shoulders, feeling welcome there unlike the ghost traces, the notion of his touch. There was so much they could hide as they were. They'd get hungrier and more numerous, more capable of eating all that she needed them to eat and ridding her world of pain. For now, though she enjoyed the hands upon her and the relaxation they brought, the little sensual shocks. These were her doing even under the influence of the charcoals, these brought her comfort and a bit of power.

She closed her eyes and let herself feel the volition she had taken back and the touch that she had brought forth on her terms. They were moving to her back, her waist, her sides as she drew them, caressing her hair and face now. They were hers and that mattered tremendously. A few days ago, she knew more about why that was and what she had lost over time but right now, there was freedom in the conjured touch she'd called for. She lay down in bed and undressed, just letting them know her and understand her as only she could understand herself.

She didn't need to see what she'd conjured at work, only to feel it. Whatever she gave, they assured her with deft and loving fingers that they would give it back. Touch could be something else now.

WHAT SHE COULD ALMOST SAY

"**I** mean, there are people like you here," said Rem.

This earned a look and Rem could immediately understand why.

"Yeah, there's a couple brothers here," said Shannon, taking another hit, "but still, you know, it's lonely."

Rem was the one making the look this time and Shannon could immediately see it was justified. She had earned it by choosing isolation. The last few days in particular she hadn't been seen much at all. She giggled inwardly knowing the dirty little secret that occupied plenty of her spare time now, those little jolts to life. Still, Rem was right. Shannon had been retreating inward, to the dorm to the page and to the comforts of the things she created, dubious as they were. She was there with Rem on the couch now though. She didn't much want a lecture but one was probably coming. People were like that.

"I think you'd be less lonely if you went literally anywhere that wasn't class or Jameson's office."

"Jameson doesn't count as company?"

Rem almost choked on the piece. She laughed and wheezed all at once.

"Depends if you listen to the gossip, bitch."

Shannon was slightly taken aback. Why would anyone think that? She was right in and out most times. Nothing happened most times. Nothing ever happened in there. Jameson was an asshole but he never really touched her. She wouldn't let him do that. She couldn't doubt it, couldn't even try. The crows were all over this moment, cawing and slobbering and flicking their tiny tongues.

"Well, lucky for your slutty, triflin' ass, I don't."

"I don't recall triflin' but otherwise, yeah, bitch, guilty as charged."

This would have been an ideal time to kiss them. There were more ideal times. Shannon's phone on the table beeped a text.

"You should check that," said Rem with a wry smile, "you're very unpopular."

"Probably a bunch of hot dads asking if it's true that you've got the clap."

"Cool," said Rem, packing the bowl again, "send them over. You can have the short one."

"Okay, good cause he's got the biggest dick."

They laughed together. Rem came close, touched her shoulder. It was nice. Shannon didn't wince, didn't get nervous. Lightly brushed Rem's thigh. It was nice. Shannon wondered why they didn't do this more often. She did not let herself ask the question for very long. She picked up the phone. Text was from Wyatt.

"It's been awhile. We should have dinner sometime."

Things weren't bad with Wyatt. Weren't quite good but weren't bad. Just sort of ran together. She cut him off about six months back. The text made her a little uneasy but that stopped pretty abruptly. She had the crows for that and they were always hungry. Still, she winced.

"You good?" Rem asked, putting a hand on Shannon's shoulder.

"Yeah," said Shannon, "why?"

"You seem like, you know…"

She resisted "I'm good", "I'm fine" and the co-conspirators thereof. She owed Rem more than that. She reached through the dark and the feathers, let them let up.

"It's from Wyatt. It's been awhile. Things ended weird, I think."

Rem sighed.

"Never liked him. Don't like his friends much either. I don't get what you saw in that douche. Like yeah, he's hot, but shit."

Shannon tried to find a damn thing she could say in his defense and nothing came up because nothing was there and nothing was possible. She didn't like the parties at BC or understand why he had to fit in with these guys. Wyatt was smart and talented and these weren't his people. Unless they were. It might have been nice to kiss Rem. This would be a good time to kiss Rem.

"Does he wanna meet up?" Rem asked, moving a little down the couch in spite of themselves.

Shannon hoped Rem wouldn't care. She felt a lot more like focusing that attention on Rem instead of on the past or what the crows were cawing out for.

"Yeah."

"You gonna do it?"

"Maybe."

"Cool."

Rem was obviously lying. Shannon could have tried them, could have fucked with them. There wasn't much that would come of that though. Shannon didn't really get playing games to fuck with people. She didn't need the leverage to feel good anymore than she needed Wyatt to feel good. She didn't bother bullshitting.

"Not really."

❦

THEY WATCHED SOME YOUTUBE STUFF. THEY HAD SOME hummus. They smoked some weed. They let the day vanish into night until Rem sheepishly parted ways with Shannon as if there was someplace else to be. Shannon wasn't trying to play but still did not let Rem know that she'd prefer if they stayed. She wasn't there yet and wasn't going to rush herself. She had something for the isolation, the numbness, the hurt. She had it in her to never really be alone. With Rem gone, she let herself melt into the couch.

She let the hands toy with her hair, rub her neck and shoulders, clasp onto her breasts. She let them down her sweatpants and into her. She let them enfold her complete, dozens of dark hands and arms that she had been drawing obsessively, now here to comfort her, to protect her and furthermore to insulate her. She faded into touch and let it bring peace and warmth to her world. She let the crows take the resonances of the text from Wyatt and the things Kemp was trying to shout through the hunger of the birds.

In the impassible field of touch, she let herself sleep and forget and for the first time in quite awhile, she let herself truly want.

MONASTERY

I n dreams, when we are somewhere, there is never a question of what forces bore us there. In dreams, when we are wandering unfamiliar corridors, there is no question of what it was that we were looking for in the first place. There was no question of why she walked through drafty halls of a monastery filled with mournful chants, funereal chants and sometimes moans of flagellant agony. This was no place for her and yet she could be no place else and she felt no desire to get out. The dust and the must and the damp aside, it was right to be here.

In dreams, we do not get lost unless lost is where we are supposed to be. We may be children abandoned at the mall and unable to find our parents but we can wander the Black Forest in all its primeval wolfhaunted terror and yet we will find the grove of trees wherein the witch's hut lies with no instruction and nothing but the need to suffer and learn at the foot of said witch at said hut. Shannon did not have to ask for help in finding the library or to decide that the library was where she was headed. The library would be found and though the cold and damp and stench were real as anything else and not just visual impressions, she thought nothing of this, or nothing of anything but the need to reach wherever it was the dream was bearing her to.

The library of this cloister should have been humble and small but instead it was stacked to the surprisingly high ceilings of this cell. Books with Latin titles bound in what occasionally looked like the hide of other, less conventional species filled this chamber. Its sole inhabitant, a sullen and gaunt monk who looked as if he had not slept for days, slumped over a desk, putting more painstaking work into the book he was scrawling.

The monk fell to his knees, surrounded by the glorious illuminated manuscripts he had created. She thumbed through the books, seeing how painstakingly they had been crafted, even as the strange symbols and perverse illustrations left her feeling uneasy. The huge shape emerged from the shadows to advance upon the supplicant and Shannon could now get a good look at it. Her eyes wandered from the text to this figure, this hulking absurdity, and she liked none of what she'd seen, less than the cackling devils of the manuscripts and less than the woeful monk who had cast aside his tools.

The shape was faceless, genderless. It had visible limbs for certain, discernible and separate fingers but lacked mouth or eyes or more or less any real definition. There were tiny hairs poking from it, emerging from moles and goiters on what were clearly patches of skin that did not belong to the same person. The tones of this fleshy monstrosity were everything from the palest, smoothest white to the most callous and elephantine grey, flesh from hundreds or maybe even thousands of creatures, some probably not even human.

It grabbed hold of the monk's face, pinching it like a grandmother teasing a child. This was odd enough but she knew what it was doing as it started to yank harder, causing the monk to let out screams of agony. It was not pinching though, no, it was peeling, grabbing this man's skin and pulling it from his face, unraveling his very flesh. She wanted to scream or to find some means of making it stop. It did not take the mass long to rip the monk's skin from his body, holding the husk and examining it by the candlelight.

She had never seen a human pelt before. She never

thought that she would witness a man separated from his skin by a monster or to see the monster so lovingly and thoughtfully examining the skin that had been removed. As the monk screamed and bled out, the face on the skin that had once belonged to him spoke.

"Was flesh! Now canvas! Flesh for my legacy!"

The flayed body turned to her, bloody, dying and forlorn. Somehow, the monstrosity and the monk knew she was here now.

"God will not forget us," the monk wailed and slid to the floor. Though her mother had been religious, Shannon had thought nothing of God or the Devil. Were there a God, he would need to be twice as cruel as any Devil. Were there a Devil, he would be an utter redundancy. In this place, she was not so sure. Eyes closed. Eyes open.

She is awake back in her bed. She is tired. She is letting out the silent scream and staring off into nowhere with eyes far too wide for one so exhausted. She wraps her arms around her chest and shakes, not knowing how she is to feel about what she has observed. A dream, but another dream that wasn't a dream. She could break those charcoals in half, relics or not, and maybe she could be free of this and not have to live with the consequences of her bad choices.

Kemp is standing at the foot of her bed. She is afraid of herself because she is not afraid of him. She hates herself because right now she is not hating him. He is hanging his head, looking almost sad, which is unlike this condescending sack of shit.

"Did you give me that dream?"

Kemp does not look at her as he replies.

"Yes. It is not my intent to deceive you. We require fore-knowledge to be truly accepted."

She heaves a sigh and wishes he could see the glare she has for him.

"I didn't say you could give me nightmares."

"No nightmares. Do you feel as if you've slept?"

She doesn't answer. She doesn't sleep until she is too tired to be awake.

❧

THERE ARE DREAMS BUT IN THE MORNING, SHE FORGETS them. She carries on as if she has not seen this. She carries on when her brain and muscles betray her. She carries on, insisting her eyes stay open and loyal and that there are not short glimpses of the monk with no skin looking at her or of the tall, ashen figure who had stood at her bedside. She sits at lunch and Rem sits with her. She tries to lie to Rem.

"I'm fine," she says, "the sativa's too speedy."

"Speed's pretty speedy too," says Rem, "something's wrong with you. I don't wanna be up in your shit but bitch, I don't want you to go."

The monk stares back from the dream that was not a dream. She tries to focus on Rem and on eating lunch. The imago will not take this moment of normality from her. She has been pretending everything was normal for too long to let that go or give that to the nightmare. She makes almost confrontational eye contact with Rem, regretting it as she melts into brown softness, comfort and things she does not want to talk or think about.

"I flushed that shit," says Shannon, "I told you. It was making me weird."

Rem nodded.

"And who told you to flush that shit?"

She could do that with the charcoals she had traded out and all of this nonsense would be over and she could sleep soundly in a room no longer touched by ghosts. She could shatter them in the palm of her hand and live happily and comfortably with Rem by her side. She could sleep comfortably without ghosts and do her paintings the way she used to and switch over to design like her mother said she should and get the fine arts out of her.

In dreams when we are somewhere, there is never a question of what forces bore us there. But in life, in waking life, we can look into comfort and we can let ourselves feel and we can be away from the things that draw us deeper into hell and then maybe we can rest easy and then maybe we can do away with the coming dark and we can have some relief and go on about our lives as if we hadn't looked into that dark and found that maybe we belonged there. So, Shannon didn't say it and later on as she cried over it, she would let the crows feast on scraps and even on this uncharacteristic moment of concern and warning that Kemp had used to bring her there.

"Thank you," said Shannon.

"I feel like I don't want to leave you alone," said Rem.

"I…"

She could flush the charcoals and tear up the drawings. She could take her paints and do the figures joining hands and delighting in human warmth and kinship. She wouldn't mind going back to painting her hopes instead of her fears and to share aspirations instead of secrets. It wouldn't be so bad to live without fear of herself or a feeling of intense separation from everyone who drifted too close. She could flush the charcoals and she could be something that felt a little bit okay and maybe that thing that felt a little bit like okay would turn into okay.

"I want you to stay here with me," she said, trying to fade the skullfaced monk from her periphery, "I know I've been weird. I can't talk about the party. Don't ask me about it."

"I won't ask you about this party," Rem said, putting a hand on Shannon's shoulder, "I promise."

Rem was beginning to put the pieces together. What they saw was repulsive.

"I'm different now," said the tear-streaked mess, blinking monsters and conjured crows from her periphery and knowing they left with great reluctance, "it's not just the work that's changing, Rem."

Rem touched Shannon's face.

"Yeah? So you think people only care for each other when

they're rolled into a ball trying not to throw up or not showing up for shit because they're afraid of seeing people?"

Maybe she did. Crows pushed out the canvas thirsting for instances of a little girl in the living room drawing and trying her damnedest not to make a sound that might set her mother off, yelling and crying and reminding her that there was no dad to keep her in order and she needed to give her mom some quiet because she had had a difficult day at the store.

"It's more than that, Rem." Shannon blinked to expel the sight of Kemp from the corner of her eyes and once more to forget the monk with no skin, the mass of flesh and the murder of charcoal crows. There was so much to say and none of it could be said.

Rem continued to stroke Shannon's face, they kept their eyes locked in spite of Shannon's desire to look away. Shannon had not altogether seen how patient and kind Rem had already been with her and had not taken in the well of patience and kindness where it had formed and what it was that kept filling it. Rem watched the tears well up again, took in the sobs and the sudden labored breathing.

"I don't need to know what you've been through. Not til you're ready. But I care about you and I'll listen when you are. It's okay. We all get scared of ourselves sometimes. You think I don't? You think I never look in a mirror and don't understand what I'm looking at? You know why I got these cuts on my arm."

She couldn't tell Rem just how many worlds apart their problems were but she could see that she mattered to someone and that there was a person out there who cared about whether she suffered or not, whether she hated herself or not and whether she could do what she needed to do. The only kindness she had felt had been that of the crows, who gathered around to peck at the thoughts that were keeping her from connecting and keeping her from putting her own hands on her friend's face.

She let the fear fade. She let the crows eat. She let herself act without the pain interspersing itself between her and the people and the objects in space that it had before. She did not need to ask what she would do if she had not been bound by a father dead on the street, by a mother who needed quiet and peace and to be left to do her best, by the hands she let on her to find some semblance of approval or connection. She did not need to ask because in this moment of liberation, still red with tears, still frustrated from lack and estrangement, she did what she would have done. She kissed Rem.

The kiss had the pressure that the Earth would have otherwise exerted. The kiss took her from a figure of charcoal to something like the aerial things that she had painted in vibrant blues, reds, yellows and greens. She went from small and powerless to someone aglow with potential in that moment. She wanted something, someone, and she acted upon it. Was this tangible? Shannon was surprised at herself, suddenly regarding that she was a being that could touch and influence and change things around her and that maybe she could want things or people or something else altogether out of life.

Then once more, fear hung suspended but unconsummated. How dare she? Shannon should be quiet. Shannon should be small. Shannon should be compliant. Shannon needs to give in or else everyone will go away. It was her job to please and her job to make sure she did nothing that caused those she wanted around her to get up and go and move on as as as… the crows pecked at old, bad things and filled their gullet with a frame of life she hadn't even borne witness to and then to the dream of that moment, a dream that reached out fat and greasy and grasping hands over the good things. But seriously, what if she had overstepped those bounds? What if she is grasping, groping, taking…

The broken kiss renewed in Rem's control. The doubts and terrors and the scraps crows hungered for could give way to Shannon being happy and Shannon feeling welcome hands and welcome lips and welcome in this world at all. The crows eating psychic scraps had done plenty but it was passion and excitement that let her carry on and let her feel someone and something. She did not doubt that the charcoals gave much of this but this kiss remained hers and this touch and warmth with someone else remained hers.

She pushed back only slightly, darting glances between father and crow and weeping self portrait and fevered composition that hanged there. She wanted Rem right now and wanted to be away from these shadows and their expectations and from the place that these creations had come out of. She wasn't sure this was possible or how far of a reach those shapes on the page really had or how far of a reach Thomas Kemp really had. She had to try. She had to keep this to herself and be able to enjoy it and other things to come without help from this magic that she couldn't understand.

"I want to go to your room, Rem."

Rem looked around the room and at the leaping wandering eye of the friend and the crush who they'd just kissed back. There was no sense in trying to squeeze out why Shannon was so fucking weird, what mattered more was enjoying Shannon's company and making Shannon happy and getting closer still. Maybe Shannon was a mess and this was a mistake but right now this felt very good. Whatever was going on would be best continued not under the scrutiny of this art, including a recent drawing of Shannon's dead father.

"I think you should," said Rem, "and you should see if you can get some studio space. Keep this stuff out of your face, so it's a little less heavy. I couldn't imagine sitting around, trying to…"

"I want to go there because I want you. I want you right the fuck now."

Down the hall felt like miles hand in hand. So many opportunities to turn back came up. She might have taken them had she not seen what she'd seen and needed what she needed.

Collages of human shapes made from genitals in various porn scenes. A giant Emma Goldman portrait. Funko pops of the Golden Girls. So much work proudly displayed. So much self right in your face. Rem's space reminded Shannon of what had made her feel so much for Rem. She wished she could adorn the walls with cocks and cunts and revolutionary rhetoric and be somebody who didn't even need to say who they were before they transcended gender and whatever it was they came from. There was surely a way to have this and she could feel what it would be to be someone who it was alright to be.

Shannon hesitated at thresholds as the unwelcome often do, though she felt welcome at this one, oddly enough. She swallowed her fear and desperation and let Rem lead her to the bed. She sat down and closed her eyes, told the crows not to fly over here and that she could be calm without them. She had to be calm without them. She was going to live without them. She had gone there to feed something that needed to be fed but she got a lot less desperate, eased into things and let them be okay. They spent this night together in each other's arms, let touch and comfort and passion prevail over doubt. They let it linger and feel right and warm then.

In the morning, there were plans, talk of a party the next week. In the morning, Shannon knew the room and Rem well enough to ask about the mysterious trunk in the corner.

"You wanna open it?" said Rem with a coy smile.

Shannon did and returned the smile, letting it grow into one of willful lechery.

"I wanna try some of these sometime."

"Please do."

PARTY

"I need you to eat my dreams," she had told the crows before bed, "it's really important, okay, guys? I need this one more thing from you."

They cawed in agreement, implying that they might just be ready to perform on command. She needed this to feel safe. She needed this so she could move on and do what she had to do today. She felt like a tremendous fuckup. Shit, it was just a party. Who the fuck got this nervous about parties? She wasn't some middle school dork going to her first dance. She'd gone to plenty of parties and had a perfectly good, sometimes too good a time. This mattered for some reason.

It didn't matter for "some reason." She ate half a bag of Goldfish crackers and washed them down with her third 'gansett'. She reiterated her needs.

"I don't know what you guys want for this but I'll give it to you, okay? I just want to feel fine for a day, okay? I felt fine for a day the other day. Then, Rem and I went to the movies and I felt fine for a fucking day again. That was two fucking days I felt fine. Is three too much to ask? I mean, fuck. I thought I made a pact with the fucking devil. I'm supposed to be feeling great, you fucking dicks. I know you're doing your job but I need you to do it harder."

She spied the ashen figure of Kemp out of the corner of her eye.

"Fuck you, no."

The ghost shuffled around the dorm room, clearly in sight, then disappeared into the wall or wherever he went. Best not to think about that before bed. And it was before bed. It was two thirty or some shit. She'd been sketching hands. She wanted to get hands down. The shapes were gaining definition and she needed them to keep gaining definition. She was going to break through and she was going to earn it.

There was another experience where she could feel Kemp moving in the dark, disquieted, desperate and wanting to tell her something. He would tell her, she wouldn't be able to stop him. In spite of his ashen complexion, Thomas Kemp was the oldest and whitest man she'd ever known and that meant a certain commitment to being heard, regardless of his audience's objection to this need and impulse. It was easy to forget sometimes what he was and the annoyance transformed itself into fear.

"I don't want to draw," she whispered.

Kemp cocked his head like a dog given a command beyond its comprehension. Servitude and torment blurred in the Libertine's body language. It wasn't a whole person anymore and it didn't give a shit what she wanted. At least it didn't need her to draw, even if it declined to explain what it wanted. Sometimes it wouldn't shut up, other times it could be terribly vague.

***

SHE WON SOME SLEEP AWAY FROM THEM, HOPING AS HER eyes shut that the crows would be there to help. She was sheltered at least in darkness, maybe the murder was surrounding her, blurring some details but she was naked in the dark, there were hands in the dark. There was laughter in the dark. Two fingers were grabbing her breasts, grabbing her between the legs. Others were stroking her side. There was whispered chatter, snickering.

Heavy breathing. A sullen Kemp shaking his head over and over, pacing back and forth. A booming, deep voice full of refinement, full of authority cut through the dark.

"It need not be like this. They told you you could not choose. I have more to give you still."

"What is this?" she screamed at Kemp, "What the fuck is this?"

"You know this," said Kemp, "you could explain."

She felt the words building her throat, a pressure, a need to explain it. It was in there, struggling to emerge and be born like so many of the things she created, like these myriad hands groping, pinching and misusing her body, probing inside her for the enjoyment of someone or something on the other end of the darkness. This moment was gestating and in dreams, it had to be born. She leaned into the pressure, fought for it.

A puff of feathers and mucus pushed up through her throat, bursting forth as she gagged on it, bent over, again, again and again letting out another mess of black plumage and bits of charcoal. Her eyes watered as she exhaled the dark, feathery mass. The bodies in the dark were drawing closer, the hands plumbing deeper. A finger was rubbing her anus. The heavy breathing from the dark persisted, louder, louder.

She awakened feeling phantom mass, awakened with a mouth full of feathers, spitting them up onto her quilt, along with masses of saliva and stomach acid and finally a strange, rounded pebble of charcoal. She knew what it was supposed to be. She knew what the dream was trying to suppress and explain at once, she knew why Kemp was direly concerned though he did not seem to display much empathy in general. This may have, in the damaged and no longer quite human psyche of the Libertine, been what passed for an act of generosity.

She wondered for a disgusting second what the ashen arms of the ghost actually felt like. When she got close to it, it seemed hot to the touch most of the time. That was a weird thought. Maybe. It was getting hard to tell what passed for strange now. The concern would fade though. The crows would eat and she would go about her life at a safe distance from whatever this was supposed to be. And then she'd go to a party with Rem and for a second, she'd be normal and Rem would be normal and everything would be cool.

❧

SHE WATCHED SOME *DOCTOR WHO* AND ATE A GIANT BOWL OF Cap'n Crunch. The weird mass of feathers and the dreams of the dark and the hands were not hurting her appetite at least. That was nice. She was grateful for that.

The crows gave big favors but it was the small clemencies that mattered this morning in the wake of that, at least as far as she could recollect. With an unexpected smile creeping across her face, she grabbed a fresh sketchbook and sat down on the couch, putting on *Planet Earth* and sparking up a morning bowl while she drew more crows.

She had had a dream of some sort that night. Kemp may have been there. She wondered if she should ask him about it but she probably didn't need to. It wasn't as if the sick fuck came when he was called anyway. She made life happen on the page, for some reason tearing out the drawings of hands she had done, now feeling very repulsed by them. Out of context body parts did that. There was something inherently creepy about how artists looked at human anatomy now that she thought about it.

Her hands, her hands, well, she drew with them. She painted with them. But they weren't meant to be functional but to be just like, aesthetic. It was like that Magritte. Ceci n'est pas une pipe. Took another hit of hers. Totally a real bowl. But hands, when you draw them, they're not tactile but they're instead they're like they're an aesthetic phenomenon. Of course when you get right down to it when you're dealing with artistic representation any creature becomes FUCK, I SHOULD WRITE THIS DOWN an aesthetic phenomenon instead of being. Like Kemp was now. Those hands, those crows, anybody when you get right down to it and you take away their, they become…

Hard exhale. Train of thought was headed someplace not cool. Couldn't do that. Not today. She needed better. Laughed her ass off about some joke she wasn't altogether sure she was in on. Some days, it was tough to feel like she'd been in on any jokes at all. She'd really rather this not be one of those. A lot of people would be there probably and she didn't know them super well and there weren't going to be too many people like too many people like too many…yeah. Rem pretty much only had white friends.

Which she'd gotten used to around here. It wasn't JP anymore. Barely six miles away but fuck, worlds. Fuckin' worlds. She went to her closet. She was worried about picking the wrong dress all of a sudden. Maybe she'd be too hot and that would be weird because she didn't know if she was going to be Rem's actual date or whatever. Rem could have had all kinds of shit going on. Like a cool shirt and some jeans, that would be good. A cool shirt and some jeans. That worked. The closet looked bigger than usual, deeper. She had enough clothes that it overwhelmed her but not enough that she'd find what was just right. She needed more stuff. She needed less stuff. She needed more time to prepare. She needed less time to freak the fuck out for no reason.

She looked at a short red dress she'd liked. Fuck yeah. She smiled at the curves and the eyes and the confidence. This would feel good and maybe it would get Rem to stick close by so it wouldn't be all awkward and shit. But this was more reassuring. This was kinda right. She took it from the closet, stroking the fabric affectionately.

The voice of Kemp resounded in her skull.

"The last time you wore this…"

CAW

She had thought Kemp had something to say. Not like it mattered much. Fucking freak. Fucking deadass freak. It was a fine dress. It was a great dress. Fuck him. Comforting darkness. Feathers around her, weed in her lungs. Gorgeous dress in her hands. Fuck Kemp and his bullshit. Fuck everyone and their bullshit. Nobody was going to ruin this day. Nobody.

"The last time you wore this…"

"The last time you…"

"The last time…"

"The last time…"

"The last…"

It was probably nothing. Probably just the weed and the stress and the feeling that she might have had a fucked up dream. Sometimes she felt like maybe he actually gave a shit about her, like there was something urgent he was working to get out but never could. She wished she could feel bad for him. A bit. She couldn't find those feelings though. What she'd found was this dress that she liked and wished she would wear more often. It had been some time since she had.

She picked up her phone, smiled at nothing. It was nice to smile at nothing.

"Psyched," she texted Rem.

❧

Rem looked hot. When they got to the Lyft, Shannon told Rem they looked hot.

"Takes one to know one," said Rem. Finger guns. Shannon would never have the confidence to do finger guns, even if, according to Rem, all pansexuals can do it. That was easy for Rem to say. Of course, most things were easier for Rem to say.

The party jitters came back. It was going to be weird. There was no telling what to expect, which was odd because she had been to many parties like this. It would be nice if every once in a while, shit wasn't difficult for no reason. That would be nice. She looked hot and Rem looked hot and it was going to be a nice night. Or an okay night. Or a pretty bad night that got better when they went back to Rem's place and fucked. It was going to be better than being dumb and crazy and fucked up over nothing.

"You okay?" Rem asked.

"Yeah."

"Cool."

"You'd tell me if you weren't, right?"

"Yeah," said Shannon as convincingly as she could. There might have been a time when Rem asked this before. And there was a weird thing in her throat and she felt like not thinking about a thing. There might have been a time like that.

She immediately jumped when she saw a blonde in a leather jacket, a bulky sweater and tight jorts. The outfit was willfully eccentric, strategically chosen to approximate a sense of taste but not expressing one at all. The thing in Shannon that wanted to be invisible was now very much afraid, since here and now that no longer was an option.

Grace had seen her, spotted fast like a predator in wait to pounce on her with sharp guilt claws and fangs honed on regrets. Fucking Grace. She'd hung out with Grace occasionally freshman and sophomore year. She went on double dates with her and her boyfriend back when Grace was dating one of Wyatt's buddies. Shannon hadn't quite been dating Wyatt so was pretty confused when Grace was so upset about the "breakup". Grace had a drink in her hand and was wobbling where she stood. This was an ill omen for sure. Grace was both good and terrible at drinking.

"Shannon! Holy shit, you went to a thing. This is fucking new. It's been so, so long. How have you been?"

"Good. I've been drawing a lot."

She could have said basically anything.

"Cool. You're a hard person to get a hold of. It's just, it's been so…"

"Yeah," said Shannon, "it's been ages."

She reached for the last time the last time she wore that dress.

The last time she wore that dress she No

The last time she wore that dress was

She had not seen Grace for maybe too long. She didn't mind it much. She was sure that she'd had a bad time last they'd seen each other. She was having a bad time now. She was tired of people giving her shit for wanting space, peace and quiet. She was just sick of these loud bitches and thirsty pseudointellectuals. That was it. If she had any doubt, the crows could do their job.

"It's just, like, you used to be a lot of fun," said Grace, draping an arm over her shoulder, "you were social and wild and you were my friend."

"I'm sorry?"

Grace began to cry and slur.

"We were such good friends and I miss you. You know? I fucking miss you."

Shannon looked around for Rem in hopes of extricating herself from this particular interaction but Rem had been detained by a few other friends. She could go and join Rem but it felt wrong somehow, presumptuous. Who was she to Rem? If she had many friends still, she would introduce Rem to them. Maybe she didn't feel like going over there because because because because nothing. She was okay. She looked good in this dress and there were people eyeing her approvingly, people who wished to know her and it would be a pleasure for them to do so. Yes.

Deep breath and dark plumage. No thoughts of the last time she'd worn that dress.

She sidled past Grace, not bothering to excuse herself or find any good reason to disengage. She found a red plastic cup and a quiet corner and let herself be fine for a bit, let a hand that nobody else could see start to gently stroke her hair. She could see Rem looking through the crowd and their eyes met. She appreciated that there was someone to whom she could give a nod to get the hell out.

But she couldn't bring herself to give the nod, admit surrender, promise Rem a world of awkwardness and trauma and walking away from too many people who couldn't accept her or simply ones she assumed could not. She wasn't going to do that to Rem.

"I've seen some of your drawings," said Dylan, "I like 'em. You do those crows. Jameson has a few in his office."

Shannon laughed.

"Yeah, I've been on a whole crow thing."

"Cool."

She killed her beer in one gulp.

"So, what are you into?"

He hesitated. It was a big question. She could see that he didn't know what she meant. She felt for him. Wanted to extract him from it. She was going to extract him from it but couldn't change the topic. Almost guilty.

"I like Metal. Lithography. Mcsweeney's."

It was scattershot. It was awkward as her. Cool.

"Cool."

"Yeah."

"Cool."

Silence again. Distance. It was nice to be quiet and alone somehow in this crowd. Even if she was supposedly in a young man's company. She lost track of the next couple hours of meaningless exchanges and attempts to give Rem all the space they or anyone could possibly need. Lost track of the ride back and deciding not to sleep at Rem's. She let the dozens of hands provide her comfort even if she winced from them and kept missing Kemp's words to her.

"The last time you wore that dress…"

She shook it off.

"Excuse me," she said to Dylan, "I think I gotta go do something."

She walked up to Rem, put an arm around her friend's waist and went in for a voracious, grasping kiss. She pulled away from the thought that it was selfish. Rem leaned into the display, grabbed a healthy chunk of Shannon's ass to the sound of hooting approval from onlookers.

"I wanna go," said Shannon, "I need to go."

Rem laughed.

"Yeah, you do."

The Lyft couldn't come fast enough. The space between them and the bed and the attention and the need could not be bridged fast enough. They made out within an inch of indecency in that Lyft, in the hallway leading to Rem's dorm, through the all-too-far distance to the bed. They descended to it, body to body, kissing more, learning each other's topologies and geography. Shannon rose from their rolling, tumbling, touching and passion, eyes suddenly fixed on a mysterious chest by the dresser. Rem smiled at Shannon.

"Feeling curious?"

She smiled back at Rem, it should have been tough but it came easy. In spite of Kemp and the nightmares and the tensions of the party, it was easy to smile back, easy to feel curious and excited about passion and touch and even love. She opened the chest, pulling out a belt with a seven inch purple dildo on it. She stroked the toy, felt its weight, shook a little at its ramifications. She soaked it with lube, vigorously rubbing it on, shivering a bit at each groove and curve.

Rem moved to the edge of the bed, ass up in anticipatory ecstasy. Shannon got behind them, leaning inward, at first unsure of the thing strapped to the belt. She eased in but soon was lost in it, soon high on the momentum she'd gathered and the gravity behind it. There was a violence that had never been in her hands before, a shudder from each thrust and control she had only felt directed at her. She was someone and something different as she worked it, devouring the sighs and screams and moans of her partner and letting the forces she had embraced and worked alongside copilot. She fucked in tandem with The Face Beneath.

She was rough but Rem backed into it, knowing that Shannon was experiencing rare moments of ecstasy and using power that had been taken away so many times. Shannon was strong and relevant in ways that had been previously impossible. It was the permission as much as the organ, rooted in her understanding of the toy, the meat, the weapon between her legs. They collapsed together in the moment of pleasure, silent as they took in what had happened between them and how much it could change both their worlds.

The next few days they went places together. They saw each other every minute they could, whispered back and forth during class. She avoided Jameson's invitations in favor of Rem's company. She wore the belt and seized the satisfaction she could from life and loving someone. Shannon was happy or trying hard enough to be happy that it mattered. But this was not what the Face Beneath was selling.

SAINT JOAN

She had grown to expect that dream and wakefulness would shuffle back and forth. Her feet had become a secondary conveyance and it was rare to see any journey cut into her memory. In power and weakness alike life is all destinations and the steps to get there, either so expedient or so far out of one's control that they might as well not have been there.

"I don't understand why you brought me here," said Shannon, intangible, ghostly and seated in an opulent Victorian carriage beside a younger, more vibrant, living Kemp, and yet somehow still seated across from the dead one. Another place she would bear witness.

The sullen, ash faced Libertine did not reply. He sat where he was and watched her, deathly silent. There were things of late that he was trying to say and she had very little idea what they were. She wanted out of here, away from what she felt was coming. It had existed in the province of rumor and she had assumed it true simply because it seemed in character for him. This did not mean she ever wanted to see it verified one way or another. There were so many people she was sure were abject pieces of shit and she did not need proof one way or the other. Was he proud of what was coming?

"I'm not impressed," she said, "I honestly don't give a fuck what you did. I know what you are and I hate you for it. Doesn't mean you can't shut the fuck up and give me the shit you promised me. I'm not here to learn from you."

Kemp the younger, and Kemp the dead did not respond. It wasn't surprising but it was still a huge pain in the ass. She flipped them both off.

"Fuck you. Fuck both of you."

The younger Kemp shouted for the carriage to stop as he spotted a slender, almost emaciated redhead clutching tight to a shawl for warmth, even as she looked down with palpable longing at the Thames and the silent fulfilment it promised. Here was a woman who could live or die and would gain little from either. She entered the carriage and the world faded into someplace else. She entered the carriage and the dream's next phase began. The ashen Kemp and Shannon stood together in a cold, sparse basement where the woman was chained beside a statue of a goatlike devil.

A great rotund manbeast, all hair and grease and perversity was down on all fours tearing the throat from a dog, looking up at her expectantly, eyes flashing with madness and terror. She was on the verge of tears but resolute, strangely resolute, through her ribs threatened to rip through her flesh, though her knees threatened to shatter and her face receded into the skeleton beneath it. The cadaver of a Whitechapel whore animate only in defiance of death watched the man's grim repast and pursed her lips, balled her sad, tiny fists.

"He is coming back for me soon and I will never be on the streets again. I will live in warmth and comfort as I have been promised. He will protect me."

These words sounded taught, forced in. These were a zealot's claims of a just and loving god, a sad and hungry girl clasping onto the last source of hope and comfort, even as this monster revealed himself before her. Perhaps she had taken him for a hallucination created by her pangs of hunger. Shannon winced, suddenly knowing what it was that the chained woman was looking at, rather, what had been brought to her.

"That's Salvatore Cresci," she whispered to Kemp, although nobody there could hear her. Kemp did not confirm. Kemp did not deny. He was not speaking, could not bring himself to do so. He was not so different from the presence here, less alive and less real. Though she knew she was one of the living, she felt hazy, connected more to these ghosts than to the flesh and blood world of this woman bound and suffering.

The great Renaissance painter Salvatore Cresci, whose boldness was praised by no less a man than Caravaggio, was in this place a hobgoblin of fevered imagination, just as Kemp the Libertine would one day become a charred, ashen ghost sulking over the deeds of his past and presenting them to her for reasons unknown. She waited there for what felt like months as the woman fought back despair and death, fed occasionally by an enigmatic woman in a black mask. She tried, over and over during these moments to get the sad, silent figure beside her to explain himself but to no more avail than the prisoner. For reasons she could not discern, the three waited out that prison sentence together.

She took solace through this eternity that whatever this was was not life, but an attempt to communicate what life had become for this woman. In this formless form she pondered what he could be attempting to teach her in this or why he had brought this poor prostitute down into this basement, her skeletal body soaked with piss and desperation. He had not shown why the masked woman or the tormenting glutton were treating her as they had and she would wait in this hell until the explanation came.

The crows would not come here to avail her of the moments of waiting, no ghosts within this world of ghosts. There were times in this basement where she swore the chained, delirious woman could catch her from the corner of her eye and was looking at her for succor. During other times Cresci, the dogeater glanced in their direction, performing for them as well. There was at least no cold and no hunger and none of the wants and needs of a physical form during the poor woman's suffering.

Time came when Shannon stopped believing she would wake from this and walk among light and life. She could still hear the chained woman insisting that Kemp would come and save her, come and end this. The ghostly Kemp beside her never affirmed that this was going to happen. She took to looking into the woman's eyes and seeing the hope wax and wane. She stopped looking away or pacing around and instead held vigil by her side. By Shannon's side, the ghostly Kemp still looking down kept watch and experienced this eternity.

When accustomed at last to the waiting, the figure of Kemp appeared seemingly from nowhere. He was young and rich and handsome as he had been, solemn as he was now, carrying with him an easel and paints which he set up right in front of her. The bound woman had been instructed not to speak to him until she was spoken to and she honored that, though it could not have been easy, even when compared to the trials she had lived through.

"I want to talk to you about faith," said Kemp to the bound woman.

She smiled hugely.

"I would like that."

Shannon cringed. She had almost forgotten the story even as she experienced it.

"Do you wish you could stop him?" she asked the ghostly Kemp.

"I'm not sure I'm allowed to think about such things," he replied.

She wondered who or what it was that did the permitting. It seemed, particularly observing something like this, that men like him did only what they wanted. Somehow with that capacity what he'd wanted to do had been this act of torture. Whatever did the permitting, he had to ask that permission in the first place, so somewhere in him the germ of an idea of treating someone like this had taken hold and he had made it real. She could not imagine in a million years using that freedom like this. For all of this and being forced to see it, she hated him more deeply than ever. She kept her eyes and ears on the younger, living Kemp though, watching him play out this aberration.

"Would you believe," Kemp asked the bound girl, "that I am capable of loving you and that all of this was love?"

"Yes," said the bound woman, "you gave me this place to live and you promised me even greater things if I would be patient and have faith. Nobody's been so kind to me. It was the Ripper or the bridge for me and here I am in the home of a very fine gentleman."

"Then let me tell you," said Kemp, "that everything I have said is a lie. You are a whore as you were and I cared nothing for you then. I took you off the street because it amused me. I left you here to die because it amused me as well."

The bound woman looked up at him, anguish overtaking her face. Eyes and mouth, outstretched, screams piercing, tears suddenly torrential. Shannon could see the agony there, the disappointment and the meticulously engineered fall to Earth. In this place, he had built her faith and love for him and made her believe he was testing her and there were better things ahead before he dashed them. He had worked these months just to get this light and this expression. The sacrifice was as much the work of art as was the painting he created. In this moment of sublime pain, Kemp made his Joan of Arc.

Shannon shook off this dream, awakening to the sound of saws as she shaved metal off a foot long pipe, sharpening it and sending sparks flying forth. She did not remember the choice to sharpen the pipe into whatever weapon she was making for whatever reason she now made it. She could have discarded it, being done with this strangeness but instead she took it home, stashing it in a cabinet. Whatever it was wasn't done yet but it was something she would need.

AN ABORTIVE TEXT

Rem,
I think I might be falling in love with you
Rem,
I think I want to be your girlfriend.
Rem,
I had a really good time
Rem,
I like you a lot
Rem,
I've got to tell you
Rem,
I
Rem,
I think
Rem,
Rem,
Hey
Hi
So
Rem, I love you
How R U?
Hey
Rem,

~~I've had a really good time but~~

~~Rem,~~

~~I like you a lot but there's a lot of complicated shit in my~~
~~life right now and I feel like I can't do a relationship. There~~
~~are so many things I want to tell you about how much I've~~
~~been through and why I'm so fucked up and how sorry I am~~
~~but I can't. I can't tell you why I can't tell you what happened~~
~~and I want to I want to so bad but I'm~~

~~Rem,~~

~~I can't do this.~~

The texts died before she could send them. She
wished the crows would feed on these anxieties.

She paced the room and the room kept getting
smaller. She made a box and then a box inside the box and
then a box inside that one. It was shrinking, closed in. Rem
and the room and life without Rem had her stuck and she
wasn't going to live without Rem and she wasn't going to live
with Rem.

Apartment turned into a quark size dot, small to her feet
and her eyes and her nerves as to the map and she, contained
within, so small that those concerns could surely not have
mattered. Who was she to think she mattered all that much as
to swat away love presented with ingratitude? If she walked
away forever, Rem wouldn't notice the dot. Surely a day or
two of distance would make her fade naturally from the imagination of her lover, lost to distance, lost to smallness and
entrapment in the box within the box within the dot, which
contained only Shannon, the dot.

She couldn't take the box. She couldn't take the thoughts
of the box and the thing she was inside of that very box. Something had to be done. Fresh air could be done even if that

meant exposing herself to the vastness, which wouldn't care enough to bother to blow her away. She put on pants. She put on a sweatshirt. She put her wallet and her keys and her phone into her pocket and she made her way to the door, though she hesitated at that threshold breathing hard for far longer than needed.

She walked out into the night.

There were lights of many buildings, many dorms, places where people who had called her friends, justly, unjustly, truthfully, falsely and she could go to the door and she could knock and say "sorry, I didn't text first, I shouldn't just drop in but" but if she picked up her phone and with that phone, she picked a friend nearby and composed a message, she would be standing in the dark and the vast, just waiting as she once again chose what to say to someone to keep them at just the right distance. It wouldn't do to do that.

It was the light of the pub that she wandered to, as Kemp had when he needed to see other faces and hear voices that weren't in his head.

She shuddered to think that she saw him and got him and resented the way he resented in his isolation and anger. It was ridiculous that she felt so isolated when somebody might be starting to love her. She shouldn't have felt like Thomas Kemp. She hated that she felt like Thomas Kemp. She hated that the light was looking harsh and the faces were looking pocked and jowly and twisted and low and not quite like a person and some were sunken and hungry and deathly and she could barely even look. She wondered how much of that could be his doing and the charcoal and the crows and the...

There was a face that she could bear to look at. There was something at least familiar, at least that much. She searched for transgressions against her and bad habits and friends of his she didn't like and could come up with almost nothing and in this place full of freaks and isolation, she needed it badly. There was a pull from the blue eyes and the freckles and the smile of recognition. He might have had bad friends for all she knew but he was a nice enough dude she supposed and she liked the way his t-shirt fit on him.

"Shannon," he said. It was nice that he remembered her from wherever. She didn't remember him from wherever, even if he was familiar. Had he only been forgotten because NO he seemed nice enough and he remembered her name from wherever and he wasn't like these bloated and lonely and needy distorted faces. There was that at least that much.

"Hey."

"It's Dean."

"I'm sorry."

He smiled even bigger.

"No worries. Of COURSE you made a bigger impression."

She smiled back. It came naturally. If she'd tried it would have hurt her face. She was grateful that he was blatantly thirsty and probably no rocket scientist. It would be easy to bar the door with this body and not let anyone or anything in at a time when she was losing her shit.

"Buy me a drink?"

He pretended to think about it, put his hand on his chin and feigned considering it. It was almost cute. It was nice that maybe he wasn't half bad. He had something like a sense of humor and some warmth and openness to him but she was sure as hell not going to let him get close enough that it would make her anxious. It was acceptable. It was easy.

"Yeah, I guess I will. What'll you have?"

"A PBR and a shot of well whiskey."

He nodded.

"For you, I'll spring for Old Crow."

In spite of herself, she laughed.

"Shit, son, save some pussy for the rest of us."

He shook his head.

"Never."

She had her boilermaker and then a second. He had three beers and a gin and tonic. He didn't seem to care for the G and T and she couldn't for the life of her figure out what he was trying to pull off. She liked that she didn't have to flirt very hard or throw out a lot of energy or ask a lot of questions. She was tired in so many ways. She had so little to give and this guy thankfully only wanted the one thing, which she wanted just as much, or at least she told herself that.

❧

THE TRIP HOME FADED FAST. THERE WAS THE BAR, A CAR door opened, a car door closed and now she was in bed with him.

"This was a mistake," she said, suddenly afraid of him and what he had planned.

She hadn't thought this through. She didn't deserve the love and happiness Rem provided but she sure as hell didn't deserve this either. Even if she did deserve this. Even if... she tried to shake off the thought. This was fucked up. She was fucked up and it was wrong to be her if this was how she wanted to carry on and maybe this was how she wanted to carry on.

He was holding onto her too tight. He was putting too much of his weight into it.

"Last time you liked it rough," he spat, eyes fixed on hers, hands clawing into her wrists, "I know you like it rough."

She shooed the crows as they started to gather around her head. Not this time. She was going to see it and remember and feel the pain. She saw the shapes barely through the slivers of her eyelids and felt the bodies, different bodies, different rhythms, different thrusts and different sizes but each not caring that she struggled and that she might have been asleep or unconscious.

"Let go of me, we're done here."

He shook his head.

"I can't believe you fucking forgot me. There was a lot going on but damn."

"Get off me!"

And she saw in the eyes of the young man on top of her that he wasn't going to stop and that he didn't care if she wanted him to and that there wasn't anything she said that would matter to him, even if he hadn't been on top in the first place. The crows flocked around above her, silently watching the scraps they ate coming back again, seeing that she was remembering the things she had worked so hard to liberate herself from. He was pounding away, ravenous, arhythmic, somewhere else entirely, trapped in her body and unable to reach out to her or him or to let either in. She remembered it was best not to struggle, best to go limp until it's done and feed the carrion to the crows that wanted it so.

Kemp stood in the corner, his ashen cock in hand, trying to make it rise, coalblazing face still full of disinterest. His jaw was slack with boredom, his body unresponsive, the voyeuristic impulse moving him none. Her eyes locked into those balefire lights and pleaded, which prompted a tilt of the head in recognition, more than she was getting from this asshole who wouldn't get off her.

"Ask and you'll receive," said Kemp, "ask and we can help."

The crows cawed out in agreement. If their barely shaken charcoal beaks could salivate they surely would. They were circling above the two ominously, hungrily as he pinched at her skin and drove over and over into her, unyielding from what he'd snorted, unyielding from the thrill of causing the hurt he had.

"Call for us," said the ashen man, "call for us."

"No!" she screamed, knowing the music next door would drown her out, knowing as she did that it would be her word against his, knowing as she did that he, the one assailing her, would not be aware enough of where he was at to judge her for this sudden outburst. It all sounded like yes to him because that was what he'd wanted to hear and what he needed to hear to stay hard enough to carry on. That was what mattered, staying hard enough to carry on, hard enough to prove he was better than every other guy this slut had let into her. How could he look them in the eyes, otherwise?

She could feel this in the way he kept at her and the way he strained, squinted and begged his body not to betray him, not to make it end too soon. She wished it would, so he could go and she would stop having to look at the figure in the corner pleasuring itself.

The crows began to gather above him. She looked up at them, wanting to shoo them away but understanding that this indignity wouldn't stop and that if she said anything, he would track her down and do it to her again. She understood that if she told anyone, it would be her fault, it would always be her fault.

It was her fault the last time that... a crow perched on her shoulder, pecking at the debris of that half formed thought that she wouldn't let in.

Two crows perched on his shoulder, their little black talons, sinking into his skin.

He winced.

"What was...what is…"

He saw it only a brief moment before the sharp, black beak plunged into his eye. He had a moment to slap it away but the pain was too much and it was again driving the sharp beak home through fragile gelatin and then yanking it from the socket.

He roared, started to pull out to find that more of them had gathered on his back and they were using the same talons and sharp beaks to tear into him.

A diabolical grin made its way onto Shannon's face. She didn't know where it had come from but she was grabbing him by the ass and pushing up to meet his cock.

"You wanted to finish, didn't you?"

He was about to scream again, when one of the flock flew into his open mouth, choking him as it pecked at his tongue with a scissor beak. Scars, cuts and tears were appearing all along his back. He struggled for breath and with all his might, pushed off her, trying to swat and escape the crows who were choking and ripping at him. Kemp stood up from the chair.

"Go to the easel," he barked at her, "capture this."

Shannon shook her head.

"I didn't mean to...what the fuck is...why am I?"

Her breaths grew rapid, short and shallow, her mind raced, which called out more crows to surround her and then to descend on the struggling young man. She didn't want to help him but she didn't want him to die. She wanted him punished but she wanted not to be the one to do it.

She wondered if she could have stopped the crows if she wanted to enough or if she wanted to at all. He was bleeding, he was struggling, he was choking as he tried to back up to the door and found that he could not.

She walked to the easel and made eye contact. With dispassionate eyes she observed his agony, his thrashing and his knowledge that life was dripping out of him and choking from existence. She looked at the wrinkling and the unpleasant shapes of the irretrievable scream, a phenomenon she had known all too well and never saw on the face of another. She had seldom seen the tyrant silence keep anyone but her from...

Crows were descending on a moment she'd witnessed only in tiny peeks through her hands, taking in the shape of five of Wyatt's friends, eating at the curtain of anxieties that had stopped her from looking at it. There was Wyatt and there was him and there were three others, each not caring that she was trying to clam up and neither move or fight. She looked on this and she looked on the assailant who was lying now on the floor, looking up at her and pleading, even as he knew it too late to do anything about it.

"Get off of him!" she shouted at the crows. The crows, unresponsive, continued to peck and tear and make him choke. She looked at them and then to Kemp and understood that she could not make them stop but perhaps he could.

"You need to call them off."

Kemp shook his head.

"You have judged him for the harm he has done. You have marked him for punishment. You have killed him and the killing was just."

"No! It was you! It was you and the charcoals and the..."

The ashen creature did not let her finish.

"This man's suffering is just. You have judged him and he dies. Save his face."

He should have died quickly. He should have fallen to the floor nice and quiet, freed her from the threat and freed her from the guilt his thrashing caused. He was contorting, struggling to expel the bird from his mouth and to tear himself away from the talons. She stood and moved to the easel. She took the charcoals in hand and looked on at his thrashing and choking and suffering and she began to draw.

She traced the lines of his agony, the wrinkles in his face and the width of his screaming mouth. She textured and shaded the glass of his eyes, the expression that was there and was fading into neutral desperation, which stood in a stark contrast to the rest of his expression, which was so big and so vivid.

Time seemed to slow around her and around him as he made that last thrash, as if to accommodate her keeping record of it. If she never finished the drawing, could he never die? She toyed with the thought but the hungry crows, too focused upon their quarry, let slip the moment of mounting, the unceremonious thrust, the thoughtless caress the observation of shape after shape through eyelid slat and yes, he had to die and yes, she had to enjoy it and yes, it was right that yes yes yes, it was right…

and he stopped. Thudded down to the floor and the last that was left of him was stiff or on the canvas.

"What now?" she asked Kemp, rising into a shout, "what do we do now? We fucking killed him!"

Kemp stood above the body and placed his hands upon it and it grew hot and fire spread, like the fire that had consumed the painter. And the fire melted flesh and the fire burnt hair to a crisp and the fire melted organs and the fire made a stench that made Shannon puke. But the fire did its job and the fire claimed the victim and the fire left nothing behind but a pile of ash. Shannon sat on the couch and cried until the moment came when she did not feel like crying.

She rose from the couch, staggered and watched as Kemp

gathered the dead man's ashes. He squeezed his own gnarled grainy hands around it and shaped it.

"Did you wonder who gathered my ashes to make those? Did you think it was a cremation?"

She did not know what to make of his words or what reply there could be. She did not know why there was wriggling under her skin. Kemp approached her and opened his hands. Inside them was a fresh piece of charcoal.

"There is no art without sacrifice."

SELF PORTRAIT: SATAN TRIUMPHANT OVER SAINT MICHAEL

The third piece of the triptych is unique in that it depicts two figures. Upon the ground, there lies a beautiful, perfect, young man, well muscled but with delicate features. He is toned and strong as an inveterate ballet dancer. From his shoulders, a pair of mangled wings jut out, an impression that what you are looking at is an angel. Standing astride him, cloven hoof on his stomach, is a gloating devil, head back in uproarious laughter. Though no other portraits exist, through the title of the painting and its provenance, art historians are clear that the satanic figure laughing at his enemy's misfortune is naturally none other than Thomas Kemp. The title of this piece, one of Kemp's most famous, is *Self Portrait: Satan Triumphant Over Saint Michael.*

PRESENTATION

Shannon paced the room. She struggled to keep her eyes off of the drawing on the easel. She was thinking she should destroy it. It would feel so good to destroy it. Even if he had been cruel to her, even if he had used her, even if he had deserved it, even if it was rare to see comeuppance come to rich, white, fratboy assholes who thought that all women on Earth were theirs thanks to manifest destiny, even if it was the right thing to do (it couldn't have been the right thing to do), the drawing was feeling dirty and wrong and terrible.

She met the wide and horrified eyes of the image she'd committed to charcoal. She had known this dread before, or something like it, though she could not have imagined the physical anguish that accompanied it. The thirsty crows were cawing but she wouldn't have it, no, she couldn't watch a man die and not look at it straight on.

"You will show them," Kemp demanded.

The fire that consumed him was bright and the room itself grew hotter as those eyes glowed. He had often made himself to be a servant in this relationship but as he glowed and burned and blustered, she feared that she had little control over him or the crows or any other sending. He had shown her some of his nature and some of his power but the heat and intensity left her sure that she had not seen its limits and she was trifling with something she should not be. She had felt this at first as she struggled not to use the charcoals and now she felt it as strong as it had been.

"I'm not going to do that," she shouted, "this is horrible. This makes me sick. I didn't want to do this."

"You must show this to them. This is the nature of the bargain you've made. You will honor it and that is that."

The Flayed Monk appeared behind Kemp, adding a palpable threat to Kemp's words. She had felt before that these entities were starting to work for her but this scene filled her with doubt. She packed the drawing and the next day she would share this handiwork.

❧

SHE STRUGGLED NOT TO SCREAM AS JAMESON UNVEILED THE drawing in class the next day, observing it from all angles. The eyes of classmates were on it, each of them capable of breaking this open and revealing what she had done.

"I love this."

The professor's hand lingered just outside the canvas. He looked as if he were going to caress that face and learn its surfaces and texture. He followed the lines and the shading, again and again, beguiled, in love, entrapped by it. He had shown some more affection and appreciation for her new work but it had never been like this. He was enthralled, moved, captivated and it had all been by her hand during a young man's last moments.

"Such a face," he said, "you've captured so much desperation and anguish in it."

That face. They would look at that face and they would see a missing student and the promises made by Kemp and the crows and whatever was behind them would be broken. Someone in class would recognize him. Someone would miss him. Someone would say something for sure. Nosering had been to a couple of Wyatt's parties so might have run into

Dean there. There were two sorority girls in the class as well and surely they had encountered him at someplace or another.

It was not so long that there would be something on the news. It would be a couple days before that. But somebody must have expected him somewhere today. They may have assumed for now that she had just seen the face and remembered it and used it for this drawing. That had to be it. It wasn't so long that they would assume she had drawn him like this because she'd seen him in such a state.

There was a sudden compulsion to tell them, even if it meant spending the rest of her life in confinement of some kind. It was an accident, if it was anything. She could not have foreseen how his life would end when she brought him home and she was defending herself. She went through the day shooing crows as she went from class to a brief visit to Jameson's office and then back to the dorm. She didn't need them to compromise her. She needed the edge. She needed to be at least a little afraid.

SHE RETURNED FROM CLASS, PACED HER DORM ROOM AND called for Kemp, who came when he was bidden.

"I showed them his face," she said, shot glass in hand, "they knew him but it was like they'd forgotten him. They were looking right at him and nobody had a word or a question or a thought for him."

Kemp shrugged.

"Why would they? He's your victim."

She felt queasy, weak, as if she could barely lift the drink in her hand.

"The fuck is that supposed to mean?"

The eyes in the ashen face burned bright again, though it was different. It looked like rage but it could have been something else. Regret? Could it have been regret? She did not like the heat in them no matter what it was.

"It means that you matter now and victims don't. Their

names and faces fade. Yours will blaze bright. This is how it has been and always will be."

"They're going to find me. The cops…"

He shook his head, surprisingly nonchalant.

"Anyone who would hurt us is one of ours."

She shuddered and thought of all the things people got away with because they were great artists. She remembered the woman in his basement and how it had not mattered what she said about him after she left. She saw the stages where people accepted Oscars on behalf of Polanski, and her mind chattered with snippets of conversations about how we must separate artist from art. There were so many to protect those men and so many who would lie for those who protected them. She trembled at the implications and yet felt a sudden warm buzz someplace she did not like to look at.

The unexamined Shannon called off the crows and looked through eyeslats at her exploitation and then to all the times she'd told herself that she could say nothing because they were men and they were rich and she could say nothing. She gave the crows the smell of his flesh burning and the puddle of nonsense that he became in those last lingering seconds of life. She fed them for days when she cried over her father while her mother, wine and cigarette in trembling hands begged for some peace and quiet, just this once, Shannon, please, Shannon, I need you to just to just to just let me think and she was small and needed someone needed HUNGRY HUNGRY and…

That was all so far away. Didn't need to be. There was Rem and there was the art and the possibilities. She had seen some things but really everyone sees things. And when the clouds parted, she understood that she wasn't so small now. If someone tried to hurt her, she could hurt them. If someone fascinated her, she could fuck them. If someone offered praise or power or peace, she could take it. Memories could be pictures in her head, highlighted or snipped out as she saw fit. So much of her had been somewhere she did not want to be and now she needn't be there. The black and the smudge and the dark and the caws and the claws could come for it.

Kemp was still there as she pulled away from it all, shaking it off, rearing up and rising from her chair. Rising from her chair to grab for the charcoals, rising from her chair to cradle them in her hand where they were vulnerable as seized testicles if she deemed it was right to crush them. Silently and from nowhere as he was wont to, the monk had slid into the room, to stop her, to aid her, to deceive her or to destroy her. The charcoals were in her hand and she could crush them and say begone or something or say her prayers or get baptized again or whatever the hell else there was.

The next question came up hard and burned all the way just as it would.

"If that's true and I feel like doing something like that again, who will stop me?"

Her answer came from the lipless, repulsive mouth of Brother Gustav.

"Only time and in the long run, not even that."

Even Kemp and even Gustav knew then to take their leave for a while.

Shannon needed some time to contemplate her first taste of true freedom.

WATCHING FROM A SAFE
DISTANCE

Shannon had just returned from Jameson's office. She brushed her teeth and sparked up a bowl, then sat down on the couch. She felt the need to untense her body, sink into someplace else, another time. She at first had to ask herself why she had this longing again, why something that had become such a big part of her week was so consistently a thing to forget. She smoked and relaxed, let the hands work her shoulders, let the crows come down.

And then she stopped asking why it was she needed to forget. The thing itself faded first and then the feeling that the thing was missing. Where void came to be, feathers and wings took up the empty and there was no need to think anything was there before the crows or that anything had to be asked. It was easy enough with these memories because there was nothing precious to hang onto.

Fingers sank into her shoulders, rubbed her feet and thighs, massaged her temples. She could drift into sleep if she wanted to but there had been nightmares, some severe enough to know the crows had worked hard to be rid of them. The edge of sleep was nice, the precipice inviting but sleep itself was a threat to stave off. She stayed in the zone of comfort and dissociation. As she lingered in this state, and let herself drift back. She searched her mind, took inventory, thinking at last that there were things she didn't want the greedy birds taking. She spotted one and let herself go there, knowing this was a stand she needed to take.

☙❦❧

SHANNON LATCHED ONTO A DAY WHEN SHE WAS FIVE AND excited about the prospect of a day among the trees and butterflies. Her father had promised that they would go for a walk through the Arnold Arboretum. She had been quiet and good, as she promised her oft-tired mother she would be. The promise of this little place right at the edge of the city, a glimpse of forest primeval full of butterflies and exotic plants and trees, secret paths they had not yet explored even after all the times they had come here.

In six months, Brandon Hernandez would be dead on the pavement, victim of a meth head's bullet and a defective vest. In six months, he would be gone from her life. The day among butterflies was a vantage from which she could observe her father's death in the line of duty.

Shannon held her father's hand as they walked past species of willow, cherry blossom and hundreds of trees from hundreds of places that she had never heard of. Birds and squirrels and animals darted from sight as father and daughter walked past. There was no asphalt here, no noise. She loved the city and would always love the city and yet, it was nice that it was not all there was in the world and that butterflies and birds converged amid unchecked growth, protected and curated by well intentioned souls.

☙❦❧

THE CROWS CROWDED ROUND THE ARBORETUM, SUBTLY AT first. No moreso than they would usually be around in such a moment. Ripping up a dead squirrel, sitting on top of a bench. Spying from the tops of trees. These could have been the crows that were already there in the first place but she knew better. She could hear in their caws what they offered and begged herself not to accept it.

"Please," she begged them, "I need this. I need to remember. There is so much I have to remember!"

She was five and sitting among trees. Her father was with her. He was a good man but she did not miss him in particular. It was nice here. And he was nice. She could tell that much. It was hard to figure out much.

NO

The fall breeze was cool and crisp. She had a blueberry donut and a lemonade Coolatta. Her dad had a bear claw and a French vanilla iced coffee. They always stopped off at the Dunkin Donuts before the Arboretum. She liked the blueberry ones. There were things just she and her mom did too but they were vaguer. She didn't hold onto them as tightly. Her mom might have texted a few weeks back. The fall breeze was cool and crisp. She had a blueberry donut and a lemonade Coolatta. She was with her dad and they were happy.

In six months, it would become impossible to do this again. She could get on the train, sure and she could sit here and be at peace and listen but she could not do it by the side of a calm, caring, smart and gentle man who loved her and wanted nothing more to keep her and the city he grew up in safe. Sooner or later, they were going to fuck him. She wanted so much to look back at the arboretum and not see her father's death. It was so little to ask and supposedly, she had made a deal with something very powerful. It was such a small request.

A blip of a moment. The image of Kemp in his study pouring turpentine over herself as if he were a painting he was stripping from the canvas of the Earth. She did not know why she was seeing this or why she had to struggle so hard to keep hold of the day at the arboretum. She was awake but half dreaming, drifting but trying so hard to fix herself in the moment. Kemp was screaming out.

"God of the blind, I cast it off, lord of forces, I revoke, I revoke…"

Brother Gustav the Flayed shook his head.

She was sitting in the studio, charcoals in hand and just trying to remember and knowing that it mattered to remember. Kemp was trying to tie this to something else, some function he felt he had to perform but tied to this moment in time. She needed to look back in the arboretum on a nice, fall day when someone who loved and believed in her was by her side because that felt like it was missing somehow, blurry somehow, traded away by her own volition or ground up in the wheels of this legacy.

It would be nice to render in pink these blossoms, in green the lushness that was soon to fade, in red, the leaves soon to perish on the ground, but that was not the medium. The medium was darkness deemed wrong by consensus of those afraid of what they could not see or would not look at close enough to determine the nuance and textures, the sinews beneath the feathers of crows, the firmness, the lines on the faces of the dying. There was something close enough to long for when she had rendered those dancers taking off and she needed now to cling to it.

"Please," she begged the crows.

"Please," she begged Kemp.

"Let me just..."

She fought for it and held on, in spite of a lingering dread that she could go through life as she was and come out with as little worth reliving as Kemp the Libertine had. She was five years old and sitting in the arboretum with her father. At least she had that.

"Keep this," he said, "I'll keep trying. I have one thing to show you and eventually, you'll have eyes for it."

She let herself sit there while she could.

AUTHORITY

Too many gallery openings lately. Jameson had pressed the importance of them and had gone out of his way to make sure she came with him through two others that week. They had been spending more time together than she cared to, left her feeling uncomfortable and dirty for some reason. Spending two hours getting ready to spend four hours standing around was a bridge too far. Especially with him.

He'd singled her out for being her and plastered his eyeballs on her tits class after class. He swatted away any notion that Sickert or Cresci or god forbid fucking Kemp were anything but saintly. He'd put his weight behind edgelords and sycophants and then now that she had fallen in with the legacy of Thomas Kemp, he treated her with a familiarity that she wanted from almost no one. Rem perhaps. But Rem never called.

It was awkward being dressed to the nines, quiet and stiff and pleasant with this trash. She broke away from Jameson the first time an old friend tried to engage him. He'd warned her before that she should stick by him and she would make some great contacts but she resisted. So much talk of sacrifice and paying dues from assholes who got what they had from other people's sweat and blood. She wondered time and again why she even agreed to do this for a guy like him.

She looked over the shades she wore so she could smoke up without anyone noticing and saw a wall of bronzed dollar bills, parts from old broken toys. Spines of pageless books. There was a message there about squandered opportunities and lost potential and the people society leaves behind but she wasn't buying it, not really. She did feel something else though, a sensation usually banished by the dulled expectations she'd lived with, muted by the voices of loud white boys in class, overshadowed by bad memories and the pain hungry flock that took care of this. Lips moved beneath her lips, guided her to the words she wanted to say aloud.

"This is bullshit," she said, not noticing the sixty something white lady beside her, the beacon of Back Bay privilege in tortoise shell glasses. She did as soon as the words came out. Fuck. Jameson had sidled further away too. She had manifested a multitude of ghosts on her account but this Karen felt a whole lot more scary. Women like this turned phonecalls into orbital strikes.

"Go on." said this Vera Wanged hipster cunt, probably shivering with pleasure at the thought of calling forth some authorities.

Something else unexpected came next.

"There's this thing about old rich white bitch art. You see it in old, rich white dude art too. There's this feeling that somebody has gone out of their way to make waste and pain and suffering. Maybe because it's a chance for the people it's made for to feel something besides Xanax and bad dick that they still had to pop up on their hind legs and beg for."

Fuck. What was that? She couldn't stop talking herself into deeper shit. These people didn't want to hear what she thought of them. They wanted to go off on a young black woman for talking out of turn and show her her place. It was hard to even talk like this in class. Here in their world, it was so much riskier. She didn't like it here but the snake had offered fruit and she took it and she could feel herself cast out into a dark night of "told you so" and "know your place".

Sooner or later, they're going to fuck us.

But she wasn't.

"You're right," said the Karen, "there's pain we'll never get. We have to find it wherever we can. We're scared that we're weak and we have no excuse for being less than we could. We have to lie like this because the alternative is unthinkable. Who we are, what we got it from…"

There was a chased by lions look in the Karen's eyes for a second, as if she knew that something had seized her and if it pleased, then it could do it again. But then a sharp edit, a blip, a skip and her face returned to its old patrician smugness as if nothing had occurred at all. Shannon was wielding a power she hadn't before. She didn't want it but she needed it. She didn't want to feel young and black and queer and invisible everywhere she went anymore. She had the chance to be seen and heard, looked at as more than an object to be discarded. She had the chance to show what was in her and what she had given life. She savored this and grew curious at its limits.

Jameson saw from across the room and approached the Karen, falling into an awkward, theatrical hug.

"Trisha! It's so great to see you two there talking. Shannon is one of my most gifted students."

The Karen, Trisha, looked Shannon's body up and down, a mercantile gaze, an appraisal that intrinsically can't be made when you consider the subject a person. She knew what the gaze was implying and resented it. She would never let the likes of Jameson touch her. She didn't do quid pro quo -- at least this was what the crows were trying to tell her. In that glance, she saw at once what was being buried and why it had to be. She wanted to get away from this right now.

"I can see that," said Trisha with a wry, disquieting smile. The thing under Shannon's face writhed, puppeteering the muscles under her jaw. It tried to shape words but she held back, momentarily too embarrassed to be angry, too disgusted to lash out. Dumb bitch wasn't worth it. Shannon could appraise too if she pleased and she was worth ten of this woman.

Jameson faked an eyeroll. Laughed and it cut.

"Please, I have a three month old. I wouldn't even have TIME. Seriously, though, her work is great. Edgy. Real. Charcoal with hard lines. The faces. They're like Goya, like Schiele, intense."

"We need more artists of color with the freedom to do work like that."

Jameson nodded, broke the hug and got another glass of champagne.

"It's been just people that look like you and me for too long."

Trisha snorted.

"Especially people that look like you."

"You should check out her work sometime. Talk to Nancy about giving her a show."

Trisha put a hand on Jameson's shoulder.

"Oh, we absolutely must."

She should have been grateful. There shouldn't have been this wince. This conversation should have needed her there but it didn't. Did it need her art or her anything to happen or was this more about them than her? Bile rose as she considered how appreciative she was supposed to be of something as simple as not actively obstructing her career. She looked around the gallery as they spoke, imagining herself on these walls and seeing the jealous girl who would be standing right where she was, feeling cheated. The price of life on those walls would be needlessly steep.

But it would be nice to be seen. So she stood where she was in silence, contemplating the feeling she'd get from being seen like this, earning the attention and acclaim that she'd given up on even before art school. She wanted to make a living and thought she'd be good enough for that. Still, she had been around students, professors and smaller openings enough that she had lowered her expectations a lot. Maybe she wouldn't have to. She beamed at the notion.

Jameson broke away from the crowd and they walked outside and had a smoke. Shannon hadn't smoked before but in the last few weeks had picked up the habit. He looked at and spoke to her with a familiarity that had confused her. They had not spent that much time alone. She had not liked or trusted him. Before the charcoals, he had torn her work to shreds. And yet smoking together under the moon with the light champagne buzz of the opening, they were close, connected. He seemed to expect her to kiss him and she expected herself to do the same. It was weird but then a lot was weird lately.

She was relieved when Jameson broke the silence, "Been thinking about the private studios. I can only give out three each year but I think you deserve this. You're special. Better than them. I get this weird feeling you could be something special and it's only right to give you what you need."

The night sky was aglow with softness and promise, the breeze like the fingers she often called forth from the canvas. She was dumbfounded by the offer and the respect behind it, unsure what the motivation was or whether it was a gift from the beings she had bargained with. It was still right though. This was still something she had worked and struggled and changed for. Was there any getting it fairly? Had anyone?

Sooner or later, they're going to fuck us.

"Thank you," she said, though she could not tell who she was thanking.

AUDACITY

Days passed slow and weeks were fast and the year was almost over and there were texts on her phone that she could not always place. Wyatt said lunch was nice. She hadn't thought she'd had lunch with Wyatt and if she had, she wouldn't have figured on it being particularly nice. She tried to recall what she would have said to Wyatt, yet whenever it coalesced, there came pecking and clouds and feathers. The moment would not be reborn when there were hungry crows to claim it. Life was fast and blurry and kept leading to things she'd fail to understand or would forget later.

Usually they led back to the studio, under the watchful gaze of many crows and a sad, dead father, in the reach of hundreds of hands. She met the freshman on one of these nights, saw him just past the fog of feelings she did not want and tried to figure out the point of this night and why it should stand out among the lost ones. She was walking down the hallway talking to this freshman she'd met. He was following her with slavish devotion and all the wideeyed affection you'd find in a puppy.

This freshman she met had some tattoos she liked, had something to give her but she had not yet determined what. They grabbed dinner at Denny's and then they decided to go elsewhere, him fidgeting all the way and struggling to find questions. The freshman could not stop looking at her except when he saw that she saw what he was looking for in her, his eyes and his reddening face would divert and find some other subject but time would come, it would always come, for that gaze to be honest. There was something in it beyond mere adoration and she enjoyed both aspects, though had little interest in sharing the young man's affection. She wasn't going to fuck him and she wasn't going to tell him that she wasn't going to fuck him because really, it shouldn't have mattered.

It was possible that like many men of many different ages that she had known, he made the assumption that if one adores someone sufficiently or wants someone sufficiently than by transit, they would reciprocate this desire. Did pies that cooled on sills leap from their perch and into hungry men's mouths? One would have thought so if they'd seen how so many men seemed to think desire worked. Were it not for the knowledge that she was so much in control, this desire would have felt intimidating, since it meant the freshman thought she wanted him very much and this is what brought him to the studio.

As they entered the studio, he stood stiffer even than he had before, more nervous and eager and afraid than he'd been when they had talked earlier. She poured him a shot of Crow as he looked around at the work she had hanging up there, the points of pride of disgust and horror alike. He was in a sparse and empty warehouse-like space, wincing at the agonized face of the man Shannon had killed.

"You like that one?" she said to the freshman. The freshman wasn't touching his drink. He was looking at the exit. There was a question now as she observed the nervous boy as to whether she had left him intimidated or actually in her fervor and her intensity and her sudden engagement, she had left him scared. In spite of herself and all of the time she'd spent scared, she didn't really mind which one it was. Were it not for the crows and their loyal cries for scrap, this would have been a concern.

"Yes," said the freshman. He touched his drink but still he did not drink it.

She circled the room, proud and predatory. If he was intimidated by that, then that was on him. It was not her fault that young men like this were often so scared of strong women. And she, in this studio space that she had barely felt like touching months before, was the strongest. He had come here to learn and she would teach. She was tempted to grab the charcoals and capture that smallness or her own intensity as she watched him and made him shrink into himself.

She pulled up her desk chair uncomfortably close to him.

"What do you like about it?"

He finally took a swig. He needed it and she needed him to need it.

"There's so much negative space but the sky is dark with these shapes. These simple forms shouldn't feel like anything special. They're really just shapes but the way you compose them and the way that one crow seems close and has that weird glint in its eye, it feels like you've captured something in this one."

She leaned in, head on folded arms.

"You're right. They're not hard to draw. You could take those charcoals and you could probably fill a canvas with crows like that."

"Yeah but it wouldn't be the same. There's so much that you capture in those crows and the way they're flying and ready to swoop and that one crow begging. It looks so real."

She tried not to laugh. She tried not to take too much pleasure in the freshman's squirm in his seat. She couldn't find it in her to be kind or gracious or patient with him though. She soaked it in and warmed herself by the heat that was pooling sweat on his face. It was cool in the studio but she was warmed by his unease. She nodded mutely, implying that he should go on and that she was waiting to be impressed. He wasn't in the classroom where he would have felt this pressure but here, it was different. She could see in him that he felt stakes rising but did not know what it was that made them rise.

"I just- I just- I really like...I'm sorry, I don't know why I'm so nervous. I guess, it's..."

She laughed.

"I know why you're so nervous," she said, the Kemp in her rising up and spreading sadistic glee, "you think you're going to get fucked tonight."

A look of fear stretched him out and wrenched eyes open. He shook his head, looked at the door, then looked back. He didn't want to flee. He wanted to flee. She could tell that he didn't like that he was found out and that he was barely entertaining the possibility. He was stuck in this moment, willing to bite off arms to extricate himself from the shame and the awkwardness and the wrong that he'd plunged himself into.

"No, I mean I...that wasn't...I don't...we met one time. You probably don't remember but it feels weird, you know, when you talk to somebody at party and they seem to think you're cool and..."

She stood up, turned her back on him.

"So, you don't wanna fuck me? What's wrong with me, huh? Don't fuck black girls? You a fucking racist? Of course you're a fucking racist. Why am I not surprised."

She couldn't let him see the smile. She had dreamed of circumstances like this and how she would act in these moments. She had known that, given the opportunity, she was too nice a person and too afraid of being seen as a bitch to actually act this way. Stay quiet, stay small, stay humble. Not today. Not here. She was surprised she didn't need to laugh into her hands. It was terribly funny.

He gulped, breathed heavy and struggled it out.

"Of course I want to fuck you. You're talented and you're smart and you're really fucking hot. Any guy would..."

She didn't need whispers from Kemp or the charcoals for the stroke of inspiration which came next. The exacto knife that she'd used to cut canvas was sitting on the desk. She picked it up and turned back around, eyes ablaze with madness, wide, predatory smile. He was ready to beg and cry and grovel for his life. She hungered for him to do so. He was squirming hard in that seat, trying to melt into a puddle that could ooze out the door. He closed his eyes.

"I'm sorry, whatever I did, I'm sorry…"

So many hands had grasped for her. So many bodies had held her down and suffocated her, leaving her struggling for freedom from underneath them and freedom from the need to be underneath them. He may not have done that yet, though for all she knew, he might have been at that party and he might have been one of the others and if he was one of the others, he deserved no better than death for what he had done or else what he would have. It would be nice to know he wouldn't get away with whatever that was.

She flicked her wrist quickly, his eyes closing and his breath stolen. He shook back and forth in his seat but it was brief. She did what she had to and it was less than she thought it had to be. There was a cut, deep and swift and unforgettable, one that saw purchase and drew blood, marking him with a gash on his cheek. He exhaled, looking at her, incredulous and waiting for the next humiliation or the final violence. He waited to hear from her that he would not get to leave.

"What?" she growled at him. "is there something you're waiting for?"

He shook his head, puffy, red with tears and scarred by the knife. Somehow, she knew that he knew. She had felt high on personal power from the very notion that someone could see that she was beyond the reach, the scope, the breadth and depth of law. But she was bigger than that. She was part of a conspiracy that had once marshalled forces against her and he could see it in his moments of weakness and fragility.

"Get the fuck out of my sight," she mumbled, though to him the invitation was loud and clear enough.

He did and the room grew cold. He opened the door and walked out and someone else walked in.

The studio was enveloped by awe. An inaudible fanfare seemed to announce the coming of something or someone of the most profound importance. She struggled not to go down to her knees but still, she did, shaking with the force of something older than anything she had ever known or could know.

Shannon had never felt herself in the presence of greatness before but was now certain she was there.

The poise, the posture, the air of command that surrounded the older man who appeared from nothing was undeniable. Handsome, upright, powerful, possessing distinguished and delicate features, he motioned for her to rise to her feet. He smiled and she was filled with warmth. She wanted him to smile at her. She needed him to approve of her. No one who saw this man would not want his approval.

"Who are you?" she asked, "Are you with Kemp?"

"You do not know me," he said, "and I have not been explained. I come to you because you are getting closer. You have big things to do."

She pushed past the awe because she had to understand. He might be angry if she did not understand. She sought to fathom this man's anger but she came up blank. The weight of it eluded even her and anger felt vast and cosmic, even if always justified.

"Are you the Devil?" she asked him, "Kemp didn't show me who gave him what he got."

The visitor shook his head.

"I am greater than God and the Devil. I come when I am called and I honor my agreements. I have built all things that you survey and I honor fellow architects. I always have."

She reached for some manner of understanding. She had seen her mother try to find something that brought order to the universe in church on Sunday, she had looked for that herself amidst the tragedy. She could see that if there was such a thing, she might well be staring at it and like so much else, it had done no favors for her and people like her, few concessions to outsiders.

"What do you want from me?" she asked, stifling every desire to ask of one who hands out power why it chose to do so as it had done.

"To claim what I will give. To put on your exhibition and make your masterwork. To be greater. I want to know what you do with this freedom. I have seen it exercised so many ways and I want to see yours."

She wanted to flee from these words, or to go back to the moment where she placed the face she'd drawn on hers and where she had drawn with Kemp's charcoals and took Kemp's miracles and by extension the miracles of this enigmatic gentleman.

"And if I refuse?"

"Then they will be given back and given out elsewhere. Someone will take it. I would prefer it be you but I am not sentimental. I am never sentimental."

She could rescind and give back what she had and go back to life as talent choked in silence as multitudes of men like Kemp thrived. She could do this or keep what was hers, even if there was no way for it to be clean. Maybe this couldn't be clean for anyone. She would see this through and keep getting louder and prouder and taking the gifts she deserved at whatever price.

"I won't refuse."

UNTITLED PIETA

The Fourth Panel of the Triptych suspends in raw potential. The Fourth Panel was made before it was made and might have always been. The Fourth Panel shows bodies unmade, hails of bullets and life coming to an end.

SOMETHING MISSING

Was there some reason Rem hadn't called?

It would have been nice to see Rem.

Hands and feathers. The sound of cawing. A deep sleep. The feel of something moving beneath her face.

What happened? She was in the studio, she knew that much. Her mind and the things around her were fragmented and decontextualized. It was harder and harder to piece things.

Blood on a sharp length of pipe. Face twitching again. Kemp was pacing back and forth through the studio.

"This is the third time," he said.

She winced, exhaling heavy over and over and over again... What was happening? Kemp was trying to tell her but the noise was too much. Cacophony of caws. Ugly shredding, ripping sounds. Fog of feathers, multiplicity of hands. Life fades again. They are trying to black out the arboretum and the day of the fateful call she overheard from the hallway. They are trying to block out something else, the pebble, smooth stone, rough touch. Voices and heavy breathing and soreness and weight, something, someone pressing her down. This was the third time she put something away in her desk but could not recognize the object. There were only the most fragmented impressions of what went on, shards of consciousness.

Daylight came screeching in, ripping her eyes open to its myriad obligations and potential tragedies. She couldn't do it. She was losing time, working the crows and phantom hands hard to devour stress. She emailed Jameson that she was skipping class to work some more. The rest was broken into bits still. She smoked a bowl. She ate junk food. She let the hands work her into frenzy. She got bored, got dressed and went to a diner. Ate lunch. With someone. Said goodbye, made plans. Blur of feathers, thirsty beaks. Let them take the doubt, the anguish, let them take the not needed. Hours of furious drawing. More hands, more crows. A hurt, betrayed face. A tall, strange figure, its expression unreadable. A feeling of twitches and squirms of facial muscle. She recalled a moment of deleting a text and letting herself drift back to the arboretum of her memory.

Night came sudden and she was at the bar. Flanagan's maybe. Grendel's Den maybe. She was talking to a skinny hipster in a Spiderman shirt. It could have been the first time. It was hard to tell lately. The rest of the conversation wasn't clear. He was in the middle of something. She didn't much care what.

"Black girls are just, like, earthier. I hope that's not racist."

"No."

A blur. Standing in the studio once again. The thing under her face crawling and writhing and shifting and digging. She shook. She tried to call off the charcoaled hands that crawled from all these canvases hanging on the walls. They were stirring and grasping and moving, swarm becoming puddle, puddle becoming tide.

The young hipster tried to scream but a hand reached up and covered his mouth. Shannon approached her desk, opened it. Feathers and talons and beaks and an inky mass of birds concealed the object, concealed the moment and the thing that came next, which fell into abortive screams. Through foggy eyes, squinting to pierce the charcoal night, she saw that the crows were eating something and this time the food was real and tangible. Ugly snaps, squishes, dirty scrapes and squelches.

And then she was back at her place, startled by the familiar figure of the Libertine.

"This is the fourth time," said Kemp.

❦

IN THE MORNING, SHANNON, LONELY, EMPTY AND UNSURE, decided that it was time to check her voicemail.

"Hey, I don't know what happened," said the voicemail, "and I know you're busy and I know you've been through a lot of shit, Shannon…"

SHE CONTEMPLATED TURNING OFF THE VOICEMAIL. THE hungry caws affirmed they'd be let down if she did. So, though she wished she could turn off the voicemail, the voicemail would not be turned off. She replayed it from the start. She did it for them as much as she did for her. Didn't seem like she was doing it much for her at all.

"…and I know you've been through a lot of shit and I just wish you'd talk about it and now I'm drunk on your voicemail like a fucking creep and I don't like it. I wanna see you, I wanna talk to you, I fucking love you and I miss you and even if you just wanted to be my friend…"

A SIGH.

"No, fuck that, don't just be my friend. But even if you just
wanted to be my friend, I want you around. Shannon, this is
fucking bullshit, okay? I miss you. You made me fucking say
that I miss you in this fucking dumb voicemail. Fuck you,
Shannon. Call me, come see me."

THERE WERE SO MANY REASONS WHY SHE WOULD HAVE
done that. It would have made her happy. It would have given
her a second to think about something besides all of the
terrible shit she knew and had been asked to sacrifice for,
whatever she was sacrificing it for or to. And she could feel
even through the gnaws and pecks and feathered obscurement
of the memories, she could feel she had been happier then and
there, as short a time ago as that might have been. As long a
time ago as that felt.

She could knock on Rem's door and tearfully pleading, half
mad from lack of touch and lack of love, and she could just say
that she had been scared and why she was scared. But she
wasn't going to. She sank into her couch, let the hands provide
her peace. She moaned while fingers brought her what she
wanted from Rem, what she wanted from anyone she could
trust. The promise of the Duke was the promise of a life where
needs could be fulfilled and she would not need to suffer for
them, nor anguish over choices that she made.

And yet suddenly, there was Kemp standing at the couch,
watching, not with any kind of perverse satisfaction but with
solemnity, patience and melancholy painted on his ashwrought
face. The crows gathered near but pulled back as he shook his
head. She disengaged the hands with an impatient huff, let the
crows fly off now.

"I don't get you," she hissed at him, "what do you fucking
want from me?"

"Read your texts," he said, "you've seen him a few times."

"Rem? Hey, Rem's not…"

Kemp shook his head.

"No. I have eyes. I'm not stupid. You've hidden something,
fed it to them so you could keep going and live without it.

Read all your texts. Remember him. It needs to mean something next time."

She pulled out the phone and shooed crows, used the strength of will that had let her keep that sweet moment as a kid sitting with her father. She followed the feel of the pebble and the dream Kemp tried to gift her. She remembered now drinking in the party at Wyatt's, how proud she was of the dress and what it did to her.

She hadn't liked his friends, the jokes they felt comfortable to make as if she wasn't there at all and the others they were comfortable enough to make because it didn't matter one way or the other. They were at once condescending and too familiar, crass and arrogant, judging her for falling into imaginary etiquette traps and making her regret reaching out and all the things she had done to open up. They were being real weird that night. Worse than usual. These absolute barbarians became pillars of society every time she opened her mouth.

One of them managed to really piss her off and as they were getting into it, she set her drink down. Even though they were assholes, they were still Wyatt's people so she was safe, even if they were a bunch of douchebags.

The pebble. The stumbling. The forgetting. She understood the weight upon her as she struggled to keep her eyes shut and the reason why she'd drawn the wall of hands that wandered over her body. She understood the pebble in her throat in the dream, the numbness, the laughter and the things she had to forget and why she forgot them. This had been the last time she'd gone to a party with him, the last time she had worn that dress. She now got what had been taken and what she was trying to get back.

Crows crowded round and she shooed them. No, not this time. She beheld herself on her knees in Jameson's offices, heard promises on his lips that had nothing to do with her work. Watched him use her again and again as she let herself fade into the ether, dissociating from her body as he made the trade he offered her and made it again, speaking lovingly to him, saying things she could not even remember herself saying, trading promises because there was no other choice. Ignoring texts and calls from Rem to join him on his arm at openings and parties she'd worked to forget. So much she didn't know.

She pinballed back and forth, spiralling through those misplaced and decontextualized nightmares, watching herself and feeling herself shut off. She tasted every word that couldn't make its way out her throat, stung her face with the salt of forgotten tears, clenched herself against all those intrusions. She had tried hard to be strong, yet could not live a life without multitudes taking what they wanted from her.

She cried in the shower. She drank and trembled and swatted greedy beasts that wanted rage she had rightly earned. Brother Gustav stood ready. The Glutton salivated with anticipation. The Face Beneath reached out and let her reshape herself as she had so many other beings. In the mirror she beheld a being that wasn't her and yet now was more herself than she had ever imagined.

WHAT YOU CANNOT WALK
BACK FROM

J ameson looked at the text with giddy anticipation. She made him a dumbass sometimes. Through the Face Beneath, Shannon watched him receive it, broadcast from his apartment into alien eyes. She listened to him lying to his all too patient wife, taking his eyes and mind off his infant son to fixate on the carnal promise that she presented to him. The time was set. She knew it was the time. She knew so much now.

She witnessed Wyatt dressing to meet up with her at this spot where she'd claimed so much power. She had given some back to him, an undue amount. She had shared her body with a man who had deemed to take it and her trust with one who deemed to shatter it. He would show up first because he would be the medium and the message and a piece she needed to make just so. She would not need to draw him. He would become the statement. There were so few limits to that which could be the statement.

The canvases stirred, so full and teeming with the malignant life they'd been given. She resented these legacies but they had only wanted to serve. They would have to be taught to serve. The Face Beneath helped her stand up straight. It bound her body in ritual garments covered in the kinds of inscrutable runes that adorned Brother Gustav's fleshbooks, clothing her from nothing in more than just the vestments of a new self. She towered with her newfound strength, queen and king and castle all in one.

The Face Beneath watched Wyatt come to the door of the studio, smelled the thirst and lack of consideration. Smelled on him the need to take again and again, the misplaced pride of ownership, even when there was nothing to back it up but the moments where he claimed with no claim at all, no real love or trust in it.

"What the fuck is this?" Wyatt asked the masked figure with the rebar strapon belt. He could hear the sound of cawing, hundreds of ravenous crows somewhere nearby. Getting closer and closer though he could see none at all. He heard a muffled laughter, a dog's bark and then a whimper. The air grew cold. Someone was tenderly running a hand across his cheek, another hand was upon his shoulder, rubbing and squeezing. He backed off from the towering creature before him. Its shadowy and unfathomable face showed no sign of anger or fear, little acknowledgement.

"What is this? What have you done with Shannon?"

"You," said The Face Beneath, "you have done so much already."

The hands were unbuttoning his shirt, reaching for his zipper, clasping his ankle. This couldn't be happening. He went limp, closed his eyes and sought to find refuge some-where where this wasn't occurring. He looked in the dark for answers and clarity, for confirmation that he was in a night-mare and proof that never came because it never could.

"Open your eyes!" cried the deep, stentorian voice, "you don't get to hide from this. You will bear witness."

Wyatt kept them open as the tall figure drew closer. He struggled to break free of their grasps, finding each time he did, more of them crawled from the canvas, skittering and swarming like insects and like the flock of crows that looked on. He almost got to exhale in relief when he heard someone had come to the door and walk in. The relief would be short lived, as would that of the lecherous art professor walking through the door.

A hulking brute of man had grabbed onto Professor Jameson as he entered, grappling him tightly, drooling on his ear, filling the man's face with the scent of rotten meat. The professor teetered rapidly on the edge of unconsciousness, watching as the mysterious masked figure put on a belt with a sharpened piece of rebar attached. The art professor, lured to the studio for the same reason Wyatt had been, tried to scream for help as the metal strapon tore into the young man. A slough. A crack. A squishing noise. A piercing shriek. Wetter, chunkier, less tolerable sounds echoed on, a cacophony of declarations that a body was being harshly used and rent open. The noises alone were enough to force the professor to double over vomiting.

The Glutton loosened his grip and went down on all fours, putting his grotesque, slavering face down into the disarticulated food, slurping thirstily, all the while masturbating hard. Jameson could take this chance to flee and get help but could not bear the sights, sounds, smells before him. Mouth agape, Wyatt was looking back at the professor, locking eyes with the last human who could help him. The thing rending his body to pieces and fucking him to death was not going to give him any respite. The dark, unfathomable face made no expression to betray that it was even enjoying itself.

"I don't know what's going on," said Jameson through snot and tears and panic, taking respite from a stomach threatening high treason once again. Behind the face, Shannon looked at the smallness and weakness of this man that she had prostrated herself before for those scraps of attention and for those vague promises of forward momentum. And when he was done with her there would be more and more but he was weak here, he had handed her the weapon that would be his undoing.

"Get his wife," she said to The Glutton with the lips of The Face Beneath, "the baby too."

Shannon pulled out of Wyatt, whose ravaged body slunk down dead and ripped up, blood, guts and excrement sliding out of him onto the studio floor. The Glutton stood up, gathered a fistful of that which leaked from Shannon's dead ex-boyfriend. It swallowed a glob of the disgusting mess before acknowledging its orders with the faintest glint of sentience in its barely human eyes.

"Please, don't," he begged, "I don't know who you are and why you're here but don't hurt my wife, don't hurt my son!"

Jameson gathered himself a second, as if something was occurring to him.

"Shannon, where's Shannon? Did you kill Shannon?"

She was surprised. It hadn't occurred to her that he might have cared. She contemplated letting him go. She had felt nice next to him that night at the opening. This man she'd hated in class she'd almost liked now. The Face Beneath wouldn't have it though. Her memories were too cruel, her heart hardening fast. She approached him, fierce and fast grabbed him by the throat, bashed his head against the wall, knocking him right out. So frail taking the strapon, so tiny when she choked and struck them. Was everything so small next to her?

"How can anyone do this?" she said to Kemp, and the ashen ghost stood before her to her south and bowed deeply.

"Power is power," he said, "I wish I could tell you. I chose to burn instead. You are hungry and so you eat but all you eat is hunger. It is the only thing Cresci could teach you. There's justice, I suppose. You could say there's that. It's as clean as you make it, no more, no less."

She hated him for this cop out. It made sense to The Face Beneath, which tried to explain it. She wished she could get her head quiet but knew this was part of the price.

"I could refuse, like you did."

The ash ghost nodded.

"You could. But there's so much to lose."

The Glutton reappeared, a well coiffed woman in her forties under his arm, unconscious. There were no bruises, no scars, no sign of violence. She could not see what he had done to get this woman from her home and though she could know simply by choosing to know, instead of this chose not to. He placed Mrs. Jameson gingerly on the floor, making a subhuman whining noise like the dogs that he had devoured in the past. Shannon could know what it was that upset him but again she opted not to, choosing not to know the warped and broken mind of the painter Salvatore Cresci.

The source of his consternation was nonetheless revealed upon the near instant arrival of Brother Gustav in the southern corner of the room. Squirming in the Flayed Monk's arms was Jameson's infant son. Cresci looked on the infant, salivating, whining again. She knew what Cresci cried out for now, beheld the pathetic monstrosity that the bargain had left behind. She was painfully aware with them all in one place that this was what she was part of. She would have to make the exhibition really count.

ETERNITY

There were nerves and then there was this. Vertigo and cosmic consequence swam through Shannon's consciousness. The moment was at hand, the opening and the show to end all shows, at least for her. Every exquisite line on the charcoal, faces of dead men may have reassured her that she had gone far beyond the Duke's expectations but it did nothing to make her feel ready for this exhibition to begin. She mounted Jameson on the wall beside the portrait of Wyatt's friend whose exquisite pain had made the professor lavish all this attention upon her, turning lust into obsession.

"Shannon," Jameson mumbled, "why am I here?"

Shannon giggled theatrically.

"Why are any of us here?"

He struggled, but it only drove the nails deeper. His eyes, only seconds ago hooded and fading, opened wide into the tableau she had built. Here was his wife, impaled to the floor, holding their child in pinned down arms. At either side of him were the portraits of the deceased Wyatt and the dead cop, rendered by Shannon in Kemp's charcoals. He was naked, spread wide, his hands and feet nailed to the wall, cruciform above her. On his forehead was a makeshift barbed wire crown. A corpulent naked man with a deerskull atop his head was looking at him, salivating profusely. Beside him was a tall shadow in a giant top hat, eyes burning with hate. A monk with no skin was on his knees praying in a language he could not recognize.

"This isn't real," Jameson said, "you drugged me."

Shannon nodded.

"I did give you some of Wyatt's rohypnol. There's a good possibility you're roofied and you're not seeing any of this but it's not likely."

Crows descended, one ripping his right nipple clean off his chest, another digging its beak in to claim and devour his left eye. He let out an inhuman screech, one echoed by both wife and child as he bled out in ways no one should. She turned her back on him and it was immensely satisfying. She had not expected applause though. She had not expected a voice from somewhere far away announcing "The exhibition has begun."

Time froze a moment and then reawakened, ushering in energies and presences long forgotten. Joy and delight. A feeling of the Earth taking pride in her. Power, safety, freedom. Eyes and adulation. Pointillistic figures, watercolored dancers and ladies and gentlemen of Victorian leisure appeared from nowhere, gathered to look and applaud, whispering amongst themselves as they did. Their eyes were wide with joy, excitement and appreciation. It took her only a moment to recognize some as figures from Seurat's park scenes, including a very bored woman walking a monkey, some as Neoclassical portraits, some as Lautrec's patrons of the Moulin Rouge. They were the epitome of propriety and jubilation, of white self satisfaction. Whites, greens, pinks...sunbleached, made of dots, made of watercolor blur, she had an audience now, attending this exposition.

Vermeer's Girl with a Pearl Earring squealed with delight as the slashed professor struggled in throes of almost death. Degas ballerinas leapt with exuberance across the room while a screaming wife appointed as the Virgin Mary begged to be freed. A corpulent Renaissance merchant not unlike the glutton smiled back at the portrait of Wyatt's dead friend.

Shannon's heart trembled with excitement and trepidation alike, her mind raced to reach the point at which this was something that could happen.

"I like it," said the bored woman's monkey from the Seurat, "I like it a lot."

Unlike in the painting, the monkey was masturbating furiously. The mother from Cassatt's The Bath was holding her child's head in the basin. A lecherous Henry the Eighth regarded her, the look on his fat, smug face one of genuine hunger. The room was full of these works of art, the legacy she was about to become one with. They were hurting themselves, hurting each other and gleefully deranged as they did so.

She had once thought her work would go unseen, the screams on canvas destined to die in the void for all eternity. She had thought the arts didn't need a young Dominican woman who wasn't quite straight and wasn't quite queer, wasn't quite an Atheist or a Communist or wasn't quite anything more than a person who had to survive and had pain to share and tragedy to endure and bad decisions behind her. The dotted gentry, the impressionist bon vivants now seemed to care about all of this, work that had ended in torture and murder and rape and revenge.

Jameson was wideeyed, screaming and begging, trying to make contact with the crowd of excited fops that had manifested before him, trying to get justice for himself, his wife, his baby. More red stains and falling meat to ruin immaculate blue robes beneath him. She met his eyes again and tried to find pity. She scanned the crowd and tried to find validation. She searched herself and tried to find something ahead. History, her own and that of art, gave her no more answers.

"I've done it," said Shannon, "I have nothing more to say than this."

"There will be other works, greater ones. So much has been taken from you and you have all that to give back," said Kemp, half pleading, "you don't know the price of stopping. I tried to get free and still, he took my very ashes. You are not finished yet."

There were indistinct conversations. The mother with child in basin shared conspiratorial whispers in Van Gogh's good ear. The picnickers in the park brayed with laughter at the pleas of the crucified professor. An undeterred Tarquin pinned Lucrece, egged on by the catalogued atrocities of the impromptu show. Looking right at it made it easier.

"I'm finished. If a million people see me putting corpses on a canvas, then nobody's any better off for it. I can only get famous for what I get away with now. There's little good left worth sharing."

"You're a fool," said Kemp, turning away. She could not see the sadness that overtook him, "you could live on forever. You could matter to so many."

"You refuse this and you die like a dog, like the bitch that you are," the Duke growled, "you return these gifts and life comes down upon you. You lose everything you've gotten."

The crows schooled around her, cawing urgently. Her father, wound oozing, pleaded with his vanquished eyes not to be let go again. She shuddered at the piercing screams of the infant in Mrs. Jameson's arms, at the indistinct moaning of the crucified professor and the muffled sobs of his savagely beaten wife. These things should have robbed her of focus or seized clarity from her but clarity had come and with it, she was resolute. It shouldn't have been like this. This could only end like this.

"It should have already happened. The fix was in. It was always in."

Kemp and Gustav and The Glutton joined the others in captive pleading. They waited, breath held back in lifeless lungs. Kemp struggled words out.

"You can't," he begged, "you can't let her."

The Duke shook his head.

"We go where we're welcome," he said and with a wave of his hand, they faded, gone from the Earth, gone to Hell, gone forever.

The heartbreak of violation. The cold and the flame of grief. The deafening thrum of rage. The choke, the stifled shriek of need. She fell to her knees as it collapsed on her, as it twisted and reshaped her mind that had broken and mended so many times already before the legacy and the Duke had found their ways into there. She kept her quivering hands tight on the bloodied exacto knife as she let it overcome her. There were sirens in the distance already, as if every cop on the planet had her name whispered in their ear at once. Maybe they had. Slow became fast, lost time renewed. The Duke filled once prophetic eyes with the sight of a police car en route.

When the cop finally arrived and the door burst open, she knew she could have thrown up her hands and come in quiet and still she would not live. She knew she could beg for her life and still she would not live. She could scream out that her father was a cop killed on duty or try to explain that this was not what it looked like but what she created here was enough to turn stomachs and make people doubt a just god. There were dozens of cops, entering the studio, shouting indistinguishable commands that she could not follow under the best of conditions let alone these, then opening fire. She may once have been shrouded from earthbound authority but that time had gone, she had relinquished it freely and chosen the weight over the freedom of unrepentant violence and a liberation from mercy. She chose the bullet that flew into her head. It should have worked quickly but it would take forever, giving her time to think about all she'd lost, all she refused.

❧

IT DID NOT MATTER IF IT WAS ONLY HER DYING MIND THAT told her that the dark shape of her father was walking off the canvas. There would be no more consequence if he wasn't than if he was and while she could choose, he was and that was well enough. In this moment, he stepped through bullets, fatal wound oozing eternal black. He could not soak up the bullets, real or not, no more than he could have when he was alive but still in this place between moments, the image of the dead man held onto his daughter and shared this drawn out, yawning second, a snapshot, a semblance of life that maybe no one could see.

"I'm sorry," said the shape, "they fucked us again. You knew they'd fuck us."

She looked in his agonized, violated eyes, saw what was taken. Saw longing for a life he couldn't get back. She looked then to the cops who'd shot her, sent the slow bullet into her head. He deserved better. She deserved better.

"Please," came the breathless whisper of Thomas Kemp, "please."

She reached out from this petrified moment, made to torture her for refusing a gift. In charcoal, in feathers, in pain and desperation, her will etched a single word on the bullet in her head, called to her benefactor. She did not expect him to see it or to be receptive. The word was "wait" and all things would and all things could. The tower of infernal authority returned to the studio, the Duke came with thundering fanfare of slavering fallen angels and accompanied by the shape of wild beasts that man's frightened ancestors had carved on the walls of their caves, tiger and wolf and bison and terrorbird crudely wrought, looking on as their lord passed judgment on whether the shot could be unshot.

"Yes," said the Duke to the body half doubled over, to the woman almost lost to a comet of misplaced matter suspended above her world, "I can wait. It is the weak who cannot wait."

"I want to do right with this, it's supposed to be mine and there's so much blood."

There was laughter among the cave paintings in attendance.

"Yes," said the Duke, "there is always so much blood. Should it be yours then?"

"I could destroy all of this and I don't know how much I would miss."

Bullet tip pressed cerebellum, fire and shred and hate but it did not progress. It was still as that damn park, still as the glacial cops, still as the party, still as the bath, still as the tell-tale O'Keefe cattleskull suspended in sky above, still as the cracked aristocrat smile, still as the dances that would never be dances, still as the beastheaded gods in the tombs where they were engraved to watch creatures no more likely to rise up and walk off.

"Give it to me, everything they weren't ready for and wouldn't know what to do with" she said, "not going to die this time. It's not come due yet."

The Duke nodded.

"Do what thou wilt."

And it came to her. She could. She could shape it as she wished and she could cast aside what was good and what was evil. Kemp had refused because he'd had this to begin with and did not know what it was to be without. She knew and she began her next great work, whatever that might have been. Death would not fit her great work. She unmade her death, unweaving time itself. Sending out the bullet, pulling back the blood that was lost, wrecking inertia and mending the hole in her skull. Unbent, she stood upright and watched these new physics transpire.

❦

PUSHED BACKWARD THROUGH TIME, SHANNON'S KILLERS withdrew. Hands trembling on guns, heads pulsing, the cops now mysteriously outside trembled, grasp loosening on both weapons and reality, which was shuddering. Shannon watched from behind their eyes, privy to someone else for once, privy to the nightmares of the cruel, the horrors that the powerful and the wicked would never live under. Nobody had been even-handed when they were handing out nightmares. No hands had generously portioned out the murder between us. Tears streaked down their faces as they shook their heads "No, no, no". They'd been pushed back out and the bullets were coming with them.

Crucified Jameson froze in eternal scream. She could let it swallow, she could let it fade, she could pull the nails from his hands so he could walk upright and escape. She could make his wife forget or soothe the crying infant in her arms. But she didn't know if she wanted that, if he deserved it. She would have to pass judgment or she could choose not to judge at all. For the moment, if a moment this was, they were an exquisite sculpture, in her eyes, the end of Kemp's triptych. They could be more if she saw fit.

The fops, the aristocrats, the pigment given life, exhaled heavy, falling to their knees in prayer and supplication. Shannon stood upright now, body repaired and retinue returned. The painted attendees of the gallery awaited validation, awaited orders and wondered what was to be done with them. Another wave of goddess hand, another wave of dissent and rage, a burst of light, a primordial heat born of punishment for errant souls. Back, back to what had wrought them. A pool, a puddle, a vortex of rising paint, myriad colors that flooded the gallery and soaked every possible surface, all over Shannon's skin. Gallery had given way into an ocean where an exaltant Shannon bathed and reflected.

She surrounded the ocean with trees. She surrounded the trees with butterflies. She let them bleed and suffer as they would. She let the world before paint be what it was as she contemplated what she wanted, if there would be anything beyond where she'd found comfort. She could see that there was something after her father and that touch and art and sometimes even love had been something.

All things around her vanished save this. She could burn it, she could put an end to everything she had known before this. No longer was she concerned if it was her place. She took what was given and when she returned to the false and lonesome Earth, she would choose.

ACKNOWLEDGMENTS

To Christoph and Leza
for making this book possible.

To John Skipp
for standing by and listening as I worked through this.

To my students for their enthusiasm and support.

ABOUT THE AUTHOR

Raised on the North Shore of Massachusetts in a house half the town called haunted, Garrett Cook grew up obsessed with everything curious, monstrous and perverse as well as struggles with body image, gender role and intense trauma. He has since moved on to Portland, Oregon, where there are fewer ghosts but still a great deal of perversity. His work has appeared alongside Joe Lansdale in *Best Bizarro Fiction of the Decade*, Michael Moorcock in *Kizuna* and Jack Ketchum in *DOA III* and James Joyce in *I Transgress*. He is the winner of the Wonderland award for *Time Pimp* and an Honorable Mention in *Best Horror of the Year 7* for his story *Beast with Two Backs*. His work has been translated into Spanish, Japanese and Russian.

Follow him on Twitter @GarrettACook

Website: http://garrettcookeditor.wordpress.com

OTHER BOOKS BY GARRETT COOK

MURDERLAND

ARCHELON RANCH

JIMMY PLUSH, TEDDY BEAR DETECTIVE

TIME PIMP

Y0OU MIGHT JUST MAKE IT OUT OF THIS ALIVE

A GOD OF HUNGRY WALLS

CRISIS BOY

WE PUT THE LIT IN LITERARY

CLASHBOOKS.COM

Troy, NY

FOLLOW US

TWITTER

IG

FB

@clashbooks